About Nicola Marsh

Nicola Marsh has always had a passion for writing and reading. As a youngster she devoured books when she should have been sleeping, and later kept a diary whose content could be an epic in itself! These days, when she's not enjoying life with her husband and son in her home city of Melbourne, she's at her computer, creating the romances she loves in her dream job.

Visit Nicola's website at **www.nicolamarsh.com** for the latest news of her books.

TM

Who Wants To Marry a Millionaire?

Nicola Marsh

MILLS & BOON

First published in Great Britain 2012
by Mills & Boon, an imprint of Harlequin (UK) Limited.
Harlequin (UK) Limited, Eton House, 18-24 Paradise Road,
Richmond, Surrey TW9 1SR

ISBN: 978 0 263 22672 0

Harlequin (UK) policy is to use papers that are natural, renewable and recyclable products and made from wood grown in sustainable forests. The logging and manufacturing process conform to the legal environmental regulations of the country of origin.

Printed and bound in Great Britain
by CPI Antony Rowe, Chippenham, Wiltshire

Also by Nicola Marsh

Girl in a Vintage Dress
Deserted Island, Dreamy Ex!
Wild Nights with her Wicked Boss
Overtime in the Boss's Bed
Three Times a Bridesmaid…
Marriage: For Business or Pleasure?
A Trip With the Tycoon
Two Weeks in the Magnate's Bed

Did you know these are also available as eBooks?
Visit www.millsandboon.co.uk

TM

This one's for my writing buddies,
Fiona Lowe and Joan Kilby.
Thanks for the camping tips.
If you convinced my hero to give it a go,
there's hope for me yet!

CHAPTER ONE

'WE HAVE a problem.'

Four words Rory Devlin did *not* want to hear—especially at his first Devlin Corp Shareholders' Ball.

He glanced around the Palladium ballroom, ensuring everyone was engaged in drinking, dining or dancing, with no visible crisis in sight, before acknowledging the waiter hovering at his elbow.

'What kind of problem?'

The kid, barely out of school, took a backward step and he belatedly remembered to temper his tone. It wasn't the waiter's fault he'd been dealing with non-stop hold-ups on the Portsea project all day.

Attending this shindig was the last thing he wanted to do but it had been six months since he'd stepped into the CEO role, six months since he'd tried to rebuild what had once been Australia's premier property developer, six months of repairing the damage his dad had inflicted.

The waiter glanced over his shoulder and tugged nervously at his bow tie. 'You better see for yourself.'

Annoyed at the intrusion, he signalled to his deputy, who saluted at his 'stepping out' sign, and followed the waiter to a small annexe off the main foyer, where the official launch of the Portsea project would take place in fifteen minutes.

'She's in there.'

She?

He took one look inside the annexe and balked.

'I'll take it from here,' he said, and the waiter scuttled away before he'd finished speaking.

Squaring his shoulders, he tugged at the ends of his dinner jacket and strode into the room, eyeballing *the problem.*

Who eyeballed him back with a defiant tilt of her head, sending loose shoulder-length blond waves tumbling around her heart-shaped face.

She wore a smug smile along with a flimsy blue cocktail dress that matched her eyes.

He hoped the links around her wrists and ankles were the latest eccentric fashion accessory and not what he thought they were: chains anchoring her to the display he had to unveil shortly.

'Can I help you?'

'I'm counting on it.'

Her pink-glossed lips compressed as she sized him up, starting at his Italian handmade shoes and sweeping upwards in an all-encompassing stare that made him edgy.

'Shall we go somewhere and discuss—?'

'Not possible.'

She rattled the chains at her wrist and the display gave an ominous wobble.

'As you can see, I'm a bit tied up at the moment.'

He winced at her pitiful pun and she laughed.

'Not my best, but a girl has to do what a girl has to do to get results.'

He pointed at the steel links binding her to his prized display.

'And you think chaining yourself to my company's latest project is going to achieve your objective?'

'You're here, aren't you?'

What *was* this? Some kind of revenge?

He frowned, searching his memory banks. Was she someone he'd dated? A business associate? Someone he'd slighted in some way?

If she'd gone this far to get his attention, she wanted something. Something he'd never give, considering the way she'd gone about this.

He didn't take kindly to threats or blackmail—or whatever *this* was.

Having some bold blonde wearing a dress that accentuated rather than hid her assets, her long legs bare and her toenails painted the same silver as her chains, bail him up like this…no way in hell would he cave to her demands.

She wanted to sell him prime land? Put in a tender for a job? Supply and interior decorate the luxury mansions on the Portsea project?

Stiff. She'd have to make an appointment like everyone else. This kind of stunt didn't impress him. Not one bit.

She chose that moment to shift her weight from one leg to the other, rattling the chains binding her slim ankles, drawing his attention to those long bare legs again…

His perfectly male response annoyed him as much as the time he was wasting standing here.

'You wanted to see *me* specifically?'

'If you're Rory Devlin, CEO of the company about to ruin the marine environment out near Portsea, then, yep, you're the man.'

His heart sank. Since he'd taken over the reins at Devlin Corp six months ago he'd borne the brunt of every hippy lobbyist and environmentalist in town. None that looked quite as ravishing as the woman before him, but all of them demonstrating the same headstrong fanaticism.

Eco-nuts like her had almost derailed the company. Thankfully, he had a stronger backbone than his father, who'd dilly-dallied rather than making firm decisions on the Port Douglas project last year.

Devlin Corp had ensured the rainforest in far North Queensland would be protected, but that hadn't stopped zealot protestors stalling construction, costing millions and almost bankrupting the company in the process.

If he hadn't stepped in and played hardball he shuddered to think what would have happened to his family legacy.

'You've been misinformed. My company takes great pains to ensure its developments blend with the environment, not ruin it.'

'Please.' She rolled her eyes before focussing them on him with a piercing clarity that would have intimidated a lesser man. 'I've researched the land you develop—those flashy houses you dump in the middle of nowhere and sell for a small fortune.'

She strained against her chains as if she'd like to jab him in the chest, and his gaze momentarily strayed to hers before her exasperated snort drew his attention upwards.

'Your developments slash trees and defile land and don't give a rat's about energy conservation—'

'Stop right there.'

He crossed the room to stand a foot in front of her, feeling vindicated when she had to tilt her head back to look up at him, and annoyed when a tantalising fragrance of sunshine and fresh grass and spring mornings wrapped around him.

'You're misinformed as well as trespassing. Unlock yourself. Now.'

Tiny sapphire flecks sparked in her eyes before her lips curved upwards in an infuriatingly smug smile.

'Can't do that.'

'Why?'

'Because you haven't agreed to my terms yet.'

He shook his head, pressing the pads of his fingers against his eyes. Unfortunately, when he opened them, she was still there.

'We do this the easy way or the hard way. Easy way: you unlock yourself. Hard way: I call Security and they use bolt cutters to humiliate you further.'

Her eyes narrowed, not dimming in brilliance one iota.

'Go ahead. Call them.'

Damn, she knew he was bluffing. No way would he draw attention to her and risk the shareholders getting curious.

'Give me the key.'

He took a step closer, deriving some satisfaction from the way she inhaled sharply and wriggled backwards before he realised his mistake.

He'd wanted to intimidate her; he'd ended up being an inch away from her.

'Make me.'

Her tongue darted out to moisten her bottom lip and he stared at it, shaken to the core by the insane urge to taste those lips for himself.

Hell.

He never backed down—ever. He'd taken on every challenge thrust upon him: changing schools in his mid-teens so he could be groomed to take over Devlin Corp one day, ousting his layabout father from the CEO role, stepping up when it counted and dragging an ailing company out of the red and into the black.

She wanted him to capitulate to her demands?

As if.

'I'm not playing this game with you.'

He used his frostiest, most commanding tone. The one he reserved for recalcitrant contractors who never failed to delay projects. Predictably, it did little for the pest threatening to derail his evening.

She merely smiled wider.

'Why? Games can be fun.'

Exasperated beyond belief, his fingers tingled with the urge to throttle her.

Dragging in deep, calming breaths, he stared at the model of Portsea Point, the largest project he'd undertaken since assuming CEO duties.

He needed this project to fly. Needed it to be his biggest, boldest success to push the company back to its rightful place: at the top of Australia's luxury property developers.

If he could nail this business would flood in, and Devlin Corp would shrug off the taint his father had besmirched the company with in his short stint as CEO.

Failure was not an option.

He glanced at his watch and grimaced. The unveiling would take place in less than ten minutes and he needed to get rid of this woman pronto.

Thrusting his hands into his pockets and out of strangling distance, he squared his shoulders and edged back to tower over her.

'What do you want?'

'Thought you'd never ask.'

His gaze strayed to her glossed lips again and he mentally kicked himself.

'I want a little one-on-one time with you.'

'There are easier ways to get a date.'

Confusion creased her brow for a second, before her eyes widened in horror.

'I don't want a *date* with you.'

She made it sound as if he'd offered her some one-on-one time with a nest of vipers.

'Sure? I come highly recommended.'

'I bet,' she muttered, glancing away, but not before he'd seen the flare of interest in her eyes.

'In fact, I can give you the numbers of half the Melbourne female population who could verify exactly how great a date I am and—'

'Half of Melbourne?' She snorted. 'Don't flatter yourself.'

Leaning into her personal space, he savoured her momentary flare of panic as she eased away.

'You're the one who wanted one-on-one time with me.'

'For an interview, you dolt.'

Ah…so that was what this stunt was about. An out-of-work environmentalist after a job.

He had two words for her: *hell, no.* But against his better judgement he admired her sass. Most jobseekers would apply through an agency or harass his PA for an appointment. Not many would go through this much trouble.

He crooked his finger and she warily eased forward. 'Here's a tip. You want an interview? Don't go calling your prospective boss nasty names.'

'Dolt isn't nasty. If I wanted nasty I would've gone with bast—'

'Unbelievable.'

His jaw ached with the effort not to laugh. If his employees had half the chutzpah this woman did Devlin Corp would be number one again in next to no time.

'What do you say? Give me fifteen minutes of your time and I'll ensure you won't regret it.'

She punctuated her plea with a toss of her shoulder-length blond hair and once again the tempting fragrance of spring outdoors washed over him.

He opened his mouth to refuse, to tell her exactly what he thought of her underhand tricks.

'I don't want to disrupt your Portsea project. I want to help you.'

She eyeballed him, her determination and boldness as attractive as the rest of her.

'In the marine environmental field, I'm the best there is.'

Worn down by her admirable persistence, he found himself nodding.

'Fifteen minutes.'

'Deal.'

Her triumphant grin turned sly. 'Now, if you don't mind fishing the key out of its hiding spot, I'll get out of your way.'

'Hiding spot?'

Her gaze dropped to her cleavage.

Jeez, could this evening get any crazier?

'Uh…okay.'

He'd reached a tentative hand towards her chest when she let out a howl of laughter that had him leaping backwards.

'Don't worry, I've got it.'

With a few deft flicks of her wrists she'd slipped out of her chains and kicked the ones around her ankles free.

'You set me up.'

He should have been angry, should have cancelled her interview on the spot. Instead he found himself watching her as she deftly wound the chains and stuffed them into a sparkly hold-all she'd hidden under the table, wondering what she'd come up with next to surprise him.

'I didn't set you up so much as have a little fun at your expense.'

She patted his chest. 'I snuck a peek at you earlier in

the ballroom and it looked like you could do with a little lightening up.'

Speechless, he wondered why he was putting up with her pushiness. He didn't take that from anyone—ever.

She pressed a business card into his hand and the simple touch of her palm against his fired a jolt of awareness he hadn't expected or wanted.

'My details are all there. I'll call to set up that interview.'

She slung her bag over her shoulder, the rattle of chains a reminder of the outlandishness of this evening.

'Nice to meet you, Rory Devlin.'

With a crisp salute she sauntered out through the door, leaving him gobsmacked.

CHAPTER TWO

GEMMA SHULTZ strode from the ballroom, head held high, success making her want to do a little shimmy.

With Rory Devlin boring holes in her back with his potent stare, she waited until she'd rounded a corner before doing a triumphant jig.

She'd done it. Scored an interview with the high-and-mighty CEO of the company threatening to tear her family's land apart.

An interview she had every intention of nailing.

The project to build luxury mansions out at Portsea would go ahead, she had no illusions about that, but the moment she'd heard about it she'd headed back to Melbourne with the sole intention of ensuring Devlin Corp didn't botch the beachside land she'd always loved.

Crazy, when she had no room for sentiment in her life these days, but that land had been special, the only place she'd ever felt truly comfortable in her topsy-turvy teenage world.

It was her dad's lasting legacy. A legacy her mum had upped and sold without consulting her.

Her neck muscles spasmed when she thought of her immaculately coiffed mother, who valued grooming and designer clothes and social standing, a mother who had barely acknowledged her after her dad died.

Though she'd never doubted Coral's love for her dad, she'd often wondered why the society princess had married a cabinet-maker. While her folks had seemed devoted enough, Gemma hadn't been able to see the attraction. Her dad had spent his days holed up in his workshop while Mum attended charity events or garden parties.

No surprise how Coral had viewed her passion for mudpies, slugs and rats as pets. Though she had to give her mum credit: she'd never stopped her from being a tomboy, from trailing after her dad like an apprentice. They hadn't had a lot in common but they'd been a close family; it hadn't been till later, when she'd turned fourteen and her dad had died, that a yawning chasm had developed, a distance they hadn't breached since.

People started filtering from the ballroom into the annexe and she bit back a grin. She'd bet Mr Conservative was hovering over his precious display, ensuring she hadn't scratched it with her chains.

Laughter bubbled up from within and she slapped a hand across her mouth to prevent a giggle escaping. The look on Rory Devlin's face when he'd caught sight of her chained to his display…priceless didn't come close.

She'd hazard a guess no one ever stood up to the guy. He had an air of command; when he snapped his fingers people would hop to it.

She'd been counting on the element of surprise, had wanted to railroad her way into an interview to show him exactly who he was dealing with.

Her toes cramped and she slipped out of the three-inch heels she hadn't worn in two years: the last time she'd been home and her mother had insisted she attend a charity ball for sick kids.

She couldn't fault the cause, but having to swap her denim for chiffon and work boots for stilettos had been

unbearable. Though she'd been thankful she'd kept the
outfit, for no way would she have gained access to the
Devlin Corp shindig unless she'd looked the part.

She'd timed her entrance to perfection, waiting until a
large group bearing invitations had gathered at the door
before inveigling her way in by tagging along.

No one had questioned her. Why would they, when her
mum would have forked out a small fortune for her blue
designer dress and matching shoes?

The rest had been easy, and with her objective achieved
she almost skipped down to the car park where she'd left
the battered car she'd picked up from the airport earlier
today.

She had no idea how long she'd be in town for, no idea
how long it would take to ensure her dad's land wasn't
pillaged by the corporate giant.

For now, the ancient VW would have to do. As for lodg-
ings, she had one destination in mind.

Come first thing in the morning she'd confront Coral,
demanding answers—like what had possessed her mum
to sell the one place in the world she valued most?

Gemma awoke to the pale pink fingers of a Melbourne
dawn caressing her face and a scuttling in the vicinity
of her feet.

She yawned, stretched, and unkinked her neck stiff
from sleeping on her balled-up jacket, squinting around
her dad's workshop for the culprit tap-dancing near her
toes.

Noise was good. Noise meant scrabbling mice or a curious possum. It was the silent scuttlers—like spiders—she
wasn't too keen on. She might be a tomboy but arachnids
she could do without.

A flash of white darted under the workbench and she

smiled. How many times had her pet mice got loose in here? Too many times to count, considering she'd left the door open to let them have a little freedom.

Her dad had never complained. He'd spent eons searching for them, affectionately chastising her while promising to buy new ones if Larry, Curly and Mo couldn't be found.

Her dad had been the best, and she missed him every second of every day. He'd died too young, his heart giving out before she'd graduated high school, before she'd obtained her environmental science degree, before she'd scored her first job with a huge fishing corporation in Western Australia.

Her dad had been her champion, had encouraged her tomboy ways, had shown her how to fish and catch bugs and varnish a handmade table.

He'd fostered her love of the ocean, had taught her about currents and erosion and natural coastal processes. He'd taken her snorkelling and swimming every weekend during summer, introducing her to seals and dolphins and a plethora of underwater wildlife she hadn't known existed.

They'd gone to the footy and the cricket together, had cycled around Victoria and, her favourite, camped out under the stars on his beachside land at Portsea.

The land her mum had sold to Rory Devlin and Co.

Tears of anger burned the backs of her eyes but she blinked them away. Crying wouldn't achieve a thing. Tears were futile when the only place she'd ever felt safe, content and truly at home had been ripped away. The only place where she could be herself, no questions asked, away from scrutinising stares and being found lacking because she wasn't like other girls her age.

She'd dealt with her grief at losing her dad, and now

she'd have to mourn the loss of their special place too. Not fair.

As she glanced around the workshop, at her dad's dust-covered tools, the unfinished garden bench he'd been working on when he died, his tool-belt folded and stored in its usual spot by the disused garden pots, her resolve hardened.

Now the land was gone, memories were all she had left. They'd been a team. He'd loved her for who she was. She owed him.

Unzipping her sleeping bag, she wriggled out of it and glanced at her watch. 6:00 a.m. Good. Time for her mum to get a wake-up call in more ways than one.

To her surprise, Coral answered the door on the first ring.

'Gemma? What a lovely surprise.'

Coral opened the door wider and ushered her in, but not before her sweeping glance took in Gemma's crushed leisure suit that had doubled as pyjamas, her steel-capped boots and her mussed hair dragged into a ponytail.

As for last night's make-up, which she'd caked on as part of her ruse, she could only imagine the panda eyes she'd be sporting.

A little rattled her mum hadn't commented on her appearance, or the early hour, she clomped inside and headed for the kitchen, about the only place in their immaculate South Yarra home she felt comfortable in.

'You're up early.'

Coral stiffened, before busying herself with firing up the espresso machine. 'I don't sleep much these days.'

'Insomnia?'

'Something like that.'

A flicker of guilt shot through her. She remembered her mum pacing in the middle of the night after her dad had died, but she'd been too wrapped up in her own grief to worry.

That was when the first chink in their relationship had appeared.

Coral had always been self-sufficient and capable and in control, and she had handled Karl's death with her usual aplomb. While she'd cried herself to sleep each night for the first few months, her mum would stride around the house at all hours, dusting and tidying and ensuring her home was a showpiece.

It had been a coping mechanism, and when the pacing had eventually stopped she'd thought Coral had finally adjusted to sleeping alone, but considering the early hour and the fact her mum was fully dressed, maybe her sleep patterns had been permanently shot?

'Coffee?'

Gemma nodded. 'Please.'

'Have you come straight from a work site?'

There it was: the first foray into critical territory, a territory Gemma knew too well. How many times had she borne her mum's barbs after her dad died?

Have you washed your hair?

Can't you wear a dress for once?

No boy's going to ask a tomboy to the graduation ball.

She'd learned to tune out, and with every dig she'd hardened her heart, pretending she didn't care while wishing inside she could be the kind of daughter Coral wanted.

'I actually got in last night.'

Coral's hand stilled midway between the sugar bowl and the mug. 'Why didn't you stay here?'

'I did. I bunked down in Dad's workshop.'

Horror warred with distaste before Coral blinked and assumed her usual stoical mask. 'You always did feel more comfortable out there.'

'True.'

Gemma could have sworn her mum's shoulders slumped before she resumed bustling around the kitchen.

Why did you do it? It buzzed around her head, the question demanding to be asked, but she knew better than to bail Coral up before her first caffeine hit of the day. She'd clam up or storm off in a huff, and that wouldn't cut it— not today. Today she needed answers.

'How long are you here for?'

As long as it takes to whip Rory Devlin's butt into shape.

Devlin's butt…bad analogy.

An image of dark blue eyes the colour of a Kimberley sky at night flashed into her mind, closely followed by the way he'd filled out his fancy-schmancy suit, his slick haircut, his cut-glass cheekbones.

At six-four he had the height to command attention, but the rest of the package sold it. The guy might be a cold-hearted, infuriating, corporate shark who cared for nothing bar the bottom dollar but, wow, he packed some serious heat.

She hated the fact she'd noticed.

'I'm here for a job.'

She sighed with pleasure as the first tantalising waft of roasted coffee beans hit her.

Watching her mum carefully for a reaction, she added, 'Out at Portsea.'

Coral's head snapped up, her eyes wide with fear. 'You know?'

'That you sold out? That you got rid of the one thing that meant everything to Dad?'

To me?

She slid off the bar stool and slammed her palms on the island bench. 'Of course I know.'

'I—I was going to tell you—'

'When? When I returned to Melbourne to build my dream home on that land? The home Dad helped me plan years ago? The home where I'd planned on raising my kids?'

Okay, so the latter might be stretching the truth a tad. She had no intention of getting married, let alone having kids, but the inner devastation she kept hidden enjoyed stabbing the knife of guilt and twisting hard.

Coral's lips compressed into the thin, unimpressed line she'd seen many times growing up. 'Sorry you feel that way, but you can't bowl in here every few years, stay for a day, and expect to know every detail of my life.'

Shock filtered through Gemma's astonishment. She had *every* right to know what happened to her dad's land, but she'd never heard Coral raise her voice above a cultured *tsk-tsk* if they didn't agree.

'I'm not asking for every detail, just the important ones—like why you had to sell something that meant the world to me.'

Fear flickered across Coral's expertly made-up face before she turned away on the pretext of pouring coffee.

'I—I needed the money.'

She spoke so softly Gemma strained to hear it.

Coral—who wore the best clothes, used the most expensive cosmetics and lunched out daily—needed money?

'You've got to be kidding me,' she muttered, sorrow and regret clogging her lungs, making simple inhalation impossible.

She wanted to explain why this meant so much to her, wanted her mum to understand how she'd travelled the world for years, never feeling as sheltered as she did at Portsea.

She wanted her mum to truly comprehend the vulnerabilities behind her tough-girl exterior, the deep-seated need for approval she'd deliberately hidden beneath layers of practised indifference.

She wanted her mum to realise her anger was about the loss of another childhood security rather than not being consulted.

She opened her mouth to speak but the words wouldn't come. Not after all this time. Not after the consistent lack of understanding her mum had shown when she'd been growing up. Why should now be any different?

When Coral turned around to face her she'd donned her usual frosty mask.

'I don't question your financials; I'd expect the same courtesy from you.' Coral handed her some coffee with a shaky hand, making a mockery of her poise. 'You're welcome to stay here as long as you like, no questions asked, because this is your home. But I won't tolerate being interrogated like a criminal.'

Instinctively Gemma bristled—until she realised something. She valued her independence, lived her own life and answered to no one. Including the mother she rarely visited. How would *she* feel if Coral landed on her doorstep demanding answers to sticky questions? She'd be royally peed off.

Some of the fight drained out of her and she gave a brisk nod, hiding behind her coffee mug. Besides, the damage was done. The land was sold and nothing could change that. She'd be better off focussing on things she could control, like ensuring Devlin Corp respected the beach while they built their mansion monstrosities.

'There's a spare key behind the fruit bowl.' Coral patted her sleek blond bob, an out-of-place, self-conscious gesture at odds with her air of understated elegance. 'I know we haven't always seen eye to eye, Gemma, but I'm glad you're here.'

By the time she'd recovered from her shock and whispered, 'Thanks...' Coral had sailed out of the room.

CHAPTER THREE

Rory flipped the rough-textured business card between his fingers. Recycled paper, no doubt, but there was nothing second-hand about the information staring him in the face.

He'd had the company's PI run a background check on Gemma Shultz last night, after she'd thrust her business card in his hand and exited his display like a queen.

He had to admit the results of the investigation surprised him as much as the woman had last night. She wasn't some crackpot lobbyist, hell-bent on delaying his project or, worse, ruining it.

Gemma Shultz was the real deal.

He ran his finger down the list: qualified as an environmental scientist at Melbourne University, spent a year at a major fishing company in Western Australia, specialising in marine conservation, two years working for a beachside developer in Spain, and the last few years freelancing for seaside construction companies keen on energy-saving and protecting the planet.

Impressive.

Not a hint of scandal among the lot: no throwing herself in front of bulldozers, no chaining herself to trees, no arrests for spray-painting corporate headquarters or flinging paint at fur-wearers.

Thank goodness. Bad enough she'd blackmailed him into giving her an interview. The last thing he needed was for the media to get a whiff of anything untoward.

His dad had done enough while he'd been in charge, gracing the covers of magazines and the front pages of newspapers with a constant parade of high-profile women while living the high life.

It was a pity Cuthbert Devlin—Bert, to his friends, and there had been many hangers-on—had been more focussed on squandering money than on running the company entrusted to him.

Rory shuddered to think what would have happened if Bert hadn't abdicated in favour of chasing some model to Europe, though he had a fair idea.

Devlin Corp would have been driven into the ground and his grandfather's monumental efforts in building the company from scratch would have been for nought. And what *he'd* been trained to do from his teens would have meant nothing.

He still couldn't understand why Bishop Devlin had handed the reins to his recalcitrant son—not when he'd been groomed for the job for so long. Until his grandfather had explained he needed to give Bert a chance to prove himself, to see if his son was made of sterner stuff.

Rory loved his dad, faults and all, but he couldn't understand why anyone would pass up the opportunity of a lifetime to run a major company.

A small part of him had been glad his dad had botched the top job, because he'd known it was only a matter of time till he got his chance. Now he had that chance no way would he let anything derail him—including a smart-mouthed, intelligent environmental scientist with seawater in her blood.

His intercom beeped and he hit the answer button. 'Yes, Denise?'

'Gemma Shultz to see you.'

'Send her in.'

He threw her business card into the dossier and snapped it shut. Armed with more information than last night, he was prepared for a confrontation: on *his* terms. When the sassy blonde sauntered through his door he'd be ready.

Until the moment his door opened, she stepped into his office and his preparation of the last few minutes evaporated.

His gut inexplicably tightened at the sight of her in a staid black trouser suit and a basic white business shirt. Nothing basic about the way she wore it, though. The top two buttons were undone to reveal a hint of cleavage, and her fitted trousers accentuated her legs. Legs that ended with her feet stuck into work boots.

And what were those God-awful dangly things hanging from her ears? Dolphins? Whales? Burnished copper fashioned into cheap earrings that did nothing for her plain outfit.

His mouth twisted in amusement. Gemma Shultz was nothing if not original. She wore an off-the-rack outfit, no make-up, ugly shoes and horrid earrings. Yet she intrigued him.

He couldn't fathom it.

She'd blackmailed her way into this interview and that had had his back up from the start. He didn't like having his authority questioned, didn't like some upstart environmentalist bulldozing her way in with unethical tactics, but what made it infinitely worse was he couldn't for the life of him fathom why he'd agreed to this meeting.

What was it about this woman that had him so tetchy?

'We meet again.'

Rather than offering her hand for him to shake, she surprised him again by shrugging out of her jacket and draping it over the back of a chair, making herself completely at home. And making his hands clench with the effort not to yank it off the chair and insist she put it back on again, so he wouldn't have to notice the faint outline of a lace bra beneath the semi-transparent white cotton of her blouse.

Weren't environmentalists supposed to wear hessian sacks and hemp bracelets and dreadlocks?

Annoyed at his reaction, he mentally slashed her interview allotment by five minutes. The sooner he got rid of her, the sooner he could get back to what he did best. Building the best luxury homes Melbourne had ever seen.

'Considering your tactics last night, you left me no choice.'

A smug smile curved her lips, and in that moment he knew that whatever came of this meeting Gemma Shultz could become the bane of his existence if he let her.

'I half expected you not to follow through on your promise of an interview.'

'I always keep my promises.'

He crossed his arms, recognised his defensiveness, and immediately uncrossed them. Only to find his hands itching to reach across the desk and see if her hair felt as silky-soft as it looked.

Damn, what was *wrong* with him?

She was nothing like the perfectly polished women he dated, with their trendy fashions and manicures and cleverly highlighted hair. Women who wouldn't be caught dead in a cheap suit and work boots. Women who wore diamonds for earrings, not copper marine life. Why the irrational buzz of attraction?

'Your fifteen minutes has been cut to ten. Start talking.'

Unfazed by his curtness, she pointed to his computer. 'By now I'm sure you've researched me and found a virtual plethora of information. So how about we skip the formalities and cut to the chase?'

Intrigued by her forwardness, he nodded. 'Which is?'

'I want you to hire me for the Portsea project.'

'And I want to buy the island next to Richard Branson's—but, hey, we don't always get what we want.'

Her eyes narrowed at his levity.

'I'm the best in the business. Give me a month on the project and I'll ensure every home you build is energy-efficient while maintaining viability in the surrounding environment and ensuring the beach is protected.'

'I've already had consultants look over the project—'

'Hacks.'

She leaned forward and planted her palms on his desk, her chest temptingly at eye level.

'You're a smart man. You know in the construction business it's the bottom dollar that counts. That beach? Last on the priority list. Which is why you need me. I incorporate scientific knowledge with environmental *nous*.' She straightened, shrugged. 'I'm a specialist in the marine field. You'd be a fool not to hire me.'

After the public debacle his father had made of the Port Douglas project, the company and himself, if there was one thing guaranteed to push his buttons it was being seen as stupid.

He stood so fast his chair slammed into the filing cabinet behind him, and he leaned across his desk—within strangling reach.

'I can assure you, Miss Shultz, I'm no fool. You've had your say. Please leave.'

She didn't recoil or flinch or bat an eyelid and his admiration notched further.

'Not till you've interviewed me.'

She sat, crossed her legs and rested her clasped hands on one knee.

'You promised me an interview so start asking questions.'

Stunned by her audacity, he shook his head. 'I can call Security.'

'You won't.'

Her blue eyes grew stony as she met his stonewalling gaze head-on. 'I've done my research too. You're new to this job. You want the best for Devlin Corp. Let's cut the small talk and use my remaining minutes here wisely.'

He fell into his seat and rubbed his forehead, where the beginnings of a headache were stirring.

Fine, he'd play this her way. He'd go through her little game for the next five minutes, then he'd personally escort her out and slam the door on headstrong, pushy women once and for all.

'Why don't you go ahead and tell me why a successful, headhunted, environmental scientist who has worked around the world wants to work on a Devlin Corp project?'

For the first time since she'd strutted in he glimpsed uncertainty as she tugged on an earring, before she quickly masked it with a toss of her hair.

'I like to diversify. The size of a project isn't important to me. It's the probable impact on the surrounding environment. And the Portsea project captured my attention for that reason.'

Her eyes glittered with unexpected fervour as she sat forward, her hands waving around to punctuate her words. 'Portsea's a gorgeous spot. Beaches along the Mornington Peninsula are special. You can't just dump a fancy-schmancy housing development in the middle of it and hope for the best.'

Increasingly frustrated that she saw him as some dollar-grabbing corporate raider, he had to cut this short.

'Contrary to your belief, Devlin Corp doesn't *dump* anything. When we take on a project of this magnitude we do extensive environmental studies—'

'Done by consultants. So you've said.'

She waved away his explanation, leaving him gob-smacked for the second time in twenty-four hours.

'I'm not besmirching your company's reputation. All I'm asking for is forty-eight hours to head out to the site, collate my findings and present them to you.'

'That's all?'

She ignored his sarcasm, beaming as if he'd agreed to share CEO duties with her.

'I promise you won't regret it.'

'I already do,' he muttered, thinking he must be mad to contemplate giving in to her demands.

But something she'd said rang true: he'd hired consultants previously used by his dad, and while he couldn't fault their findings he had to admit environmental outcomes weren't his area of expertise.

The consultants presented their findings, he went ahead with the project regardless, and while no red flags had jumped out at him, how well had the consultants studied how the land lay, so to speak?

He had an expert in the field sitting in front of him, offering her services for two days. Businesswise, he'd be a fool to pass up expertise of that magnitude. Personally, he wanted to boot her out before she coerced him into anything else.

'What do you say?' She held up two fingers. 'Two days is all I'm asking for.'

'If I agree to this—' her grin widened and he held up a hand to rein her in '—and it's a big *if* at this stage, how much are you charging?'

She leaned forward as if to impart some great secret.

'For you? Free.'

He reared back. He'd learned from a young age that if something looked too good to be true it usually was.

'What's the catch?'

She shrugged. 'No catch.'

He glimpsed a flicker of uncertainty in her eyes, the pinch around her mouth, the fiddle with her earring.

'Here's the deal. If you tell me the truth about why this is so important to you, I'll give you two days.'

She paled and he almost felt guilty for holding her over a barrel. Almost. For all the grief she'd put him through he should rejoice he'd finally gained the upper hand. No one got the better of him, but in twenty-four hours this woman had come close.

Indecision warred with yearning, before she finally sagged into her chair, the fight drained out of her.

'My family owned that land.'

There she went again, flooring him without trying.

'We bought it from the Karl Trust.'

She gnawed on her bottom lip. Her vulnerability was softening the hard shell he'd erected around his heart. Not from any grand passion gone wrong but for the simple reason he didn't have the time or inclination for a relationship.

He dated extensively, squiring women to corporate events and charity balls and the theatre. But dating and getting involved in a relationship were worlds apart and he liked to keep it that way. He had one love in his life— Devlin Corp—and it suited him fine.

'Karl Shultz was my dad. The land had been in his

family for a few generations, in trust. It meant a lot to us—him.'

Her slip-up told him all he needed to know. This land had personal value to her, which made him wonder why she'd let it be sold in the first place. Financial liability, most likely, but it wasn't his place to question her personal status.

'I get it. This land meant something to you and you want to ensure it's treated right.'

She clasped her hands so tight her knuckles stood out. Her reluctance to discuss anything deeper than superficialities was obvious.

'Something like that.'

She clamped her lips shut to stop herself from saying more but he'd heard enough.

'I'm a stand-up guy, Miss Shultz, and I value honesty. Especially in business.'

He held out his hand for her to shake. 'You've got yourself forty-eight hours to do your worst.'

Her answering smile made something unfamiliar twang in his chest.

'Thanks, you won't regret it.'

She placed her hand in his, her callused fingers skirting along his palm and creating a frisson of electricity that disturbed him as much as the urge to hold on longer.

'And call me Gemma. I have a feeling we'll be seeing a lot more of each other before this project is through.'

He opened his mouth to correct her, to reiterate it was two days only, but as she shook his hand and smiled at him as if he'd announced she'd won the lottery he couldn't help but think seeing more of her might not be such a bad thing after all.

CHAPTER FOUR

As the elevator doors slid open on the ground floor, and Gemma stepped into the elaborate glass-and-chrome foyer of Devlin Corp, she wrinkled her nose. The place was lit up like a Christmas tree, despite the gorgeous sun outside, and she'd hazard a guess those lights weren't dimmed at night. What a waste of electricity.

Not to mention the fancy flyers lying in discreet piles on strategically placed tables—way to go with conserving trees—and enough water coolers to irrigate an entire African village.

Maybe once she'd finished with the Portsea project good old Rory would let her overhaul his business.

Considering his perpetually bemused expression whenever she was around, she doubted it.

Exiting the glass monstrosity, she skipped down the marble stairs onto bustling Collins Street.

She'd hustled her way into that interview using bold tactics, and she intended on continuing to bombard Mr Conservative from left field.

He'd read up on her, from that folder sitting in front of him that he'd tried to slide under a pile of documents when she'd entered.

She'd expected nothing less from a go-get-'em businessman in his position, but he'd surprised her with his intuition. He'd picked up on why the land was important to her and laid out a little blackmail of his own.

He'd left her no choice but to come clean about her reasons for wanting to be involved, but rather than criticism she'd seen understanding in those perceptive blue eyes.

He'd understood. Surprising. It made her like him a tad. Enough to wonder why a rich, successful, good-looking guy in his early thirties—her research had been thorough too—wasn't engaged or married or in a relationship.

She'd seen only a few internet hits of him in the glossies or newspapers. A guy like him should have had loads printed in the gossip columns, but there'd been surprisingly little bar a few pictures of the requisite arm-candy blondes/brunettes/redheads—stick-thin women in *haute couture* accompanying him to various corporate events.

For the CEO of Australia's biggest luxury property developer, she'd expected more enlightening hits. Interesting.

As she threaded her way through the corporate suits rushing down Collins Street, with everyone in a great hurry to get where they needed to be, she took the time to look around. It had been years since she'd strolled through her home city. Her flying visits usually consisted of work and a quick obligatory visit with her mum.

As much as she loved Melbourne's beautiful gardens and trams and café culture, she'd never really felt at ease here. Attending a private girls' high school had exacerbated her alien feelings. She'd had few friends once the girls had discovered she enjoyed windsurfing and rock-climbing and camping more than sleepovers and manicures and make-up.

Throw in her love of physics and chemistry over art and literature, of participating in soccer games rather than tittering on the sidelines watching the local boys' school, and her classmates' shunning had been ensured.

She'd pretended she didn't care—had blissfully retreated to Portsea on the weekends, where she could truly be herself in a non-judgemental environment that nourished rather than criticized. But after her dad died and her relationship with her mum went pear-shaped, the insecurities her mother fed at home had festered at school, leaving her emotionally segregated from everyone.

She'd learned to shelter her emotions and present a blasé front to the world. A front that thankfully had held up in Rory Devlin's intimidating presence and gained her an opportunity to pitch. She had complete confidence in her abilities and knew once he'd heard her presentation he'd hire her.

Besides, she thought he had a soft spot. She'd seen the shift from cool businessman to reluctantly interested when she'd mentioned her family had owned the Portsea land. Who would've thought the guy had a heart? It humanised him and she didn't like that. Didn't like how it added to his appeal. He was a means to an end, nothing more.

The fact she hadn't been on a date in months had to be the reason she'd noticed how his eyes reminded her of a Santorini sky, how his lips would tempt a nun to fantasise.

When they'd shaken hands her fingers had tingled with the residual zap, making her wonder what he'd do with those strong, masterful hands in the throes of passion.

Not good to be thinking along those lines. Not good at all.

She loved her job, threw herself into it one hundred percent, but moving from place to place had consequences: she didn't have time to form attachments to any guy.

If she were completely honest, she didn't have the inclination either. She socialised—dinner, drinks, the occasional movie—but no one had captured her attention for longer than a few dates. Leading a transient life suited her. Moving on to the next job site gave her the perfect excuse to not get emotionally involved.

Garett, her regular date for functions in London, had accused her of being deliberately detached, of putting up barriers against a deeper relationship. Probably true. She'd switched to a new date for the next business dinner.

She'd mulled over her reluctance to pursue a long-term relationship at length, and while it suited her to blame her work, she knew deep down she wanted what her mum had had: the complete love of a man who adored and one hundred percent accepted you.

Her dad had been patient, kind, generous with his time and affection, and completely non-judgemental. He had been the one person who truly understood her, and once he'd died her mum's rejection had only served to increase her feelings of being an outcast.

The emotional walls she'd erected had been deliberate, a coping mechanism at the time, but they'd become such an ingrained part of her she didn't know how to lower them. Or didn't want to.

Letting a guy get too close, opening herself up to possible rejection again? Uh-uh. She might be many things, but a masochist wasn't one of them. Better to push them away before they shut her out. She'd learned that the hard way.

She had a brilliant job she adored, a freedom envied by her married colleagues, and the ocean—a place she could immerse and lose herself anywhere in the world. Why risk all that? No guy was worth it, not in her experience.

That buzz she'd experienced when Rory had shaken her hand? Nothing more than static from the posh rug in his office.

She bumped into a businessman, who shot her a filthy glare, and she apologised, sidestepped and picked up the pace, obliterating thoughts of a handsome millionaire— the least likely guy she'd be attracted to.

Rory stood on the crest and surveyed the endless indigo ocean stretching to the horizon.

Gemma's place.

That was how he'd started thinking of this stretch of beach, and he shook his head. He didn't have room for sentimentality in his life, and certainly not in his business, but there was something about her never-say-die attitude in regards to this land that plucked at his heartstrings.

She'd gone to extreme lengths to gain his attention, and while he didn't approve of her methods he couldn't fault her enthusiasm. This place meant a lot to her. He'd granted her request to provide him with assessment findings to humour her, but he had to admit he was curious. Curious about her scientific skills, curious about her work ethic, and curious about what she'd do once he vetoed her findings.

The project was ready to go, excavation set to commence in a month, and he had every intention of getting it done on time. Houses were sold, shareholders had invested, sub-contractors had been hired. Amendments were doable at this stage, but anything else she might come up with? Pie-in-the-sky dreams.

A gunshot made him jump and he whirled around, squinting at the road where it had come from. When a dented pale blue VW rolled over the hill, and backfired again before pulling up next to his Merc in a cloud of dust, he stifled a grin.

Of course she'd drive a beat-up old banger; though how environmentally safe a car like that was remained debatable.

She tumbled out of the car, all long denim-clad legs and red jumper, a gaudy floral scarf fluttering in the wind and her plait unravelling as she hurried towards him.

'Sorry I'm late.'

He jerked a thumb in the direction of the vehicle. 'Car trouble?'

'How'd you guess?'

'That thing belongs in a museum. Where'd you get it? Rent-a-Bomb?'

She blushed.

'You know the emissions from that can't be good for the environment?'

It was like waving a chainsaw in front of a greenie.

She squared her shoulders, her eyes flashing blue fire. 'Considering some of us aren't flush with funds like other people—' her scathing glare encompassed him and the Merc '—we make do with what we've got.'

He opened his mouth to respond and she held up a finger.

'As it so happens, they had nothing else available. Once I know how long I'm in town for I'll be chasing up something more suitable. Satisfied?'

'Immensely.'

Her eyes narrowed at his tongue-in-cheek response, but before she could flay him again he gestured to the land.

'How long since you've been here?'

'Five years.'

Her wistful sigh cut through his distraction.

'That's a long time to stay away from home.'

She angled her head away from him, but not before he'd glimpsed fleeting pain.

'Work keeps me pretty busy.'

'Same here.'

He knew exactly how many years she'd worked overseas, but hearing her audible regret only exacerbated his curiosity. If she loved her job so much, her regret must be personal. He'd bet some jerk had done a number on her.

'Melbourne doesn't hold good memories for you?'

She reared back as if he'd poked her in the eye. 'What makes you think that?'

'Your time spent away, your defensiveness.'

He expected her to clam up. So of course she did the opposite, surprising him yet again.

'There's nothing much left for me here any more.'

She sank onto a nearby log, resting her elbows on her knees, her chin on her hands. He eyed the log warily and she raised an eyebrow at his pause.

'No bull-ants, no spiders—nothing to bite your butt.'

She blushed again, the faint pink staining her cheeks highlighting the blueness of her eyes, making him forget his five-thousand-dollar suit as he sat just to be close to her.

'Bad break-up?'

She shook her head, the addictive fragrance of spring mornings and sunshine he'd smelt when they'd first met wafting over him.

'Uh-uh. I just don't fit in here.'

'What about family?'

'My mum lives in South Yarra. We catch up occasionally. It's been five years since I've been to the beach here, but I made a flying visit to Melbourne two years ago and saw Mum then.'

She made it sound as if she'd flown in to have a root canal.

'You don't get on?'

'Something like that.' Her hand gestured to the vista before them in an all-encompassing sweep. 'She never understood how special this place was. My dad and I used to camp here. We did a lot of stuff together...'

She trailed off and for one horrifying moment he thought she might cry. He didn't do tears, didn't know how to offer comfort, and he rushed on.

'I take it you didn't know she'd sold the land?'

'No.'

That one syllable held so much regret and rawness and retribution he almost felt guilty for delving.

'This means a lot to you.'

'You think?'

Her sarcasm, tinged with sadness, made him wish he hadn't probed for answers. If he'd kept this on a purely business level he wouldn't be feeling like the grinch that stole Christmas.

When it came to business, he didn't have time for a conscience. He didn't feel anything other than soul-deep satisfaction that he was doing what he'd been groomed to do: preserve his family legacy.

That was when it hit him.

Their situations were reversed. He'd been given an opportunity to continue his family legacy, to make it flourish, to stamp his flair, to make his mark.

How would he feel if his dad had run Devlin Corp into the ground or, worse, sold it off to the highest bidder? He'd be gutted. That was exactly how Gemma would be feeling.

'You came home especially for this, didn't you?'

'Yep.'

'You know I can't retract the sale or stop the project from going ahead?'

The moment the words spilled out of his mouth he wondered where they'd come from. He didn't owe her any explanations, but something in her defeated posture tugged.

'I wouldn't expect you to,' she said, derision curling her upper lip. 'I'm not some charity case.' She swivelled to face him, then fired back, 'You're a hard-headed businessman. I get it. All this? Gone. But if I can preserve one iota of this beauty, maybe the people who live here will appreciate it as much as we did.'

She ended on a little hitch of breath and leaped to her feet, dusting off a butt moulded temptingly by denim.

'Now, let's get to it.'

He stood, and before he'd realised what he was doing he placed a comforting hand on her shoulder.

'I'm willing to hear your ideas and keep an open mind.'

She allowed his hand to linger for a few long, tension-fraught seconds before she shrugged it off.

'Thanks. That's all I ask.'

She switched into business mode, the contrast intriguing him as much as her steely determination underlined with a thread of vulnerability.

He'd never met anyone like her.

The businesswomen he worked with were only intent on climbing the corporate ladder, while the women he dated were poised, polished and excessively cool.

They never fought for a cause or were passionate about what they believed in. They didn't care about the environment unless a passing shower ruined their blow-dried perfection. They rarely wore skinny jeans or paisley scarves.

They were nothing like Gemma.

'The marine ecosystems in Port Phillip Bay need to

be preserved.' Her eyes narrowed as they swept the horizon. 'Human-induced environmental changes, such as the mansions you're proposing to build along here, can contribute to the breakdown of sustainability.'

Although impressed by the passion shining in her eyes, he kept his tone light. 'You're trying to dazzle me with scientific speak.'

Her glare made him wish he'd kept his mouth shut.

'See these dunes below us? Destroying the vegetation in sand dunes lets the wind blow them away, increasing the coast's vulnerability to erosion.' She pointed to the scrubby bush a few feet in front of them. 'If you're building mansions behind us, you'll probably construct a sea wall along here.' She shook her head. 'Bad move. Seriously bad move. A sea wall built along a beach only protects the landward property, but ruins the beach by isolating sand behind the wall from the active beach system. This eventually leads to serious erosion problems, and eventually no beach exists in front of the wall...'

Her voice faded but her eyes had lost none of their spark as they pinned him with ferocious accusation.

'If this beach were left to erode naturally, without a sea wall, it would always be here.'

And her dad's legacy would last for ever. She didn't have to say it. It was evident in every line of her rigid body: in her defensive stance, her crossed arms, her upthrust chin daring him to disagree.

Her fervour, her passion for her cause was staggering.

'No sea wall. Got it.'

One eyebrow arched in imperious disbelief. 'You're mocking me?'

Considering he'd noticed her clenched fists, he wouldn't dare. 'Honestly? Your dedication is impressive but plans are in place, houses are sold, this project is going ahead.'

With or without your approval. It was a comment he wisely confined to his head.

'Houses? Don't you mean luxury mansions worth millions? Millions designed to make your precious company mega-wealthy.'

'You of all people know what land prices are worth along here. I'm just doing what any developer would do.'

'Yeah, plunder the land,' she muttered, her sagging shoulders the first sign of defeat.

'Construction is going ahead.' Feeling sorry for her, he softened his tone. 'What would you suggest to facilitate environmental conscientiousness?'

He listened carefully as she outlined her plans for solar panels and double glazing and toilets flushed by tank water, trying not to be distracted as the wind toyed with the strands escaping her ponytail and flushed her cheeks.

When she'd finished, she stared at him with an eyebrow raised in question.

'What do you think?'

'Collate your ideas, back them up with documented research and be ready to present to my project managers day after tomorrow.'

Her eyes widened in disbelief. 'You mean it?'

'I'm not in the habit of saying things I don't mean—'

She cut him off by flinging herself at him and wrapping her arms around his neck, that infernal scarf smacking him in the face.

He floundered, propriety dictating he unwind her arms and set her back, so as not to blur their business relationship. But by the time his brain processed what he should do it was too late.

His arms slid around her of their own volition, savouring her soft curves and the way she fitted into him.

He knew it was wrong, knew he shouldn't do it, but he

rested his cheek on the top of her head, buried his nose in her hair and inhaled, committing the fresh outdoor scent he'd associate with her for ever to memory.

For ever?

It was the reality check he needed, and he quickly eased away, grateful when she laughed off their embrace as if it meant nothing.

'Guess you can't fault me for exuberance.'

His terse nod belittled the special moment they'd shared and he glanced at his car, desperate to extract himself from an already precarious situation. One more moment in her 'exuberant' company and goodness knew what he'd do.

'Thanks for meeting me out here. I'll have that presentation ready for you.'

'Ring Denise and she'll schedule a time.'

'Great.'

He made a grand show of glancing at his watch, when in fact time meant nothing and he'd much rather spend the afternoon here than listen to a bunch of builders drone on about material costs.

'You go.' Her face softened. 'I want to spend a few more minutes here.'

On her own.

He couldn't give her the land back but he could give her the privacy she craved.

'Sure, see you in a few days.'

'Count on it.'

She smiled, and this time something beyond scary twisted in the vicinity of his heart.

He did the only thing possible.

He bolted.

CHAPTER FIVE

GEMMA waited until the purr of Rory's Mercedes faded before she found the nearest ti-tree and banged her forehead against it. Repeatedly. It didn't help.

She'd hoped it might knock some sense into her—or, better, eradicate the memory of flinging herself at Rory.

What had she been *thinking?*

That was the problem; she hadn't been thinking. She'd been so blown away by his offer to present her recommendations to the project managers logic had fled and she'd been running on pure emotion.

When it came to this place it had always been about emotion, and that was what hurt the most: the fact her mum hadn't realised its importance in her life—the haven it had provided to an isolated teenager. Or if she had she'd upped and sold it without consulting her regardless.

She rubbed her forehead, her rueful wince tempered by the incredible view. How many times had she camped here with her dad? Pitching tents, cooking sausages over an open fire, roasting marshmallows. Everything had been an adventure because her dad had made it so. He hadn't berated her for not brushing her hair or not wearing a dress or not playing with dolls. Her dad had understood her, and standing here in their spot she missed him more than ever.

She inhaled the briny air, its familiar tang infusing her lungs, releasing some of her residual tension. She'd always been more relaxed here, more at home. From the distinctive ti-trees to the grassy fringes, from the pristine sand to the untamed ocean, she'd never felt anything other than comfortable here. It was a feeling she could never replicate anywhere else—a feeling of righteousness, of oneness, that had been ripped away by a mother who had never understood.

Another major head-slapping moment. She'd divulged some of her family history to Rory. She should have known the familiarity and contentment of being here would loosen her lips. Her inhibitions too, going by that cringeworthy hug.

Though it hadn't been all bad. While she'd been regretting her impulsiveness, and searching for a dignified way to extricate herself and laugh it off, he'd hugged her back. That had been a bigger surprise than his offer to let her present to the team.

Having his strong arms wrapped around her, being wedged against his firm body, her nose pressed into the side of the neck, where she'd breathed in his woodsy aftershave...after the first few seconds, when the shock had worn off, she'd reluctantly, irrationally, enjoyed it.

His common sense had kicked in first and she'd braced herself for awkwardness, been pleasantly surprised when they'd moved past the moment.

The guy kept astounding her, and if she wasn't careful he'd pull a bigger surprise and actually get her to lower her defences.

Not on her agenda—and certainly not with a corporate hotshot like him—but for a second, with the recent memory of his arms around her, it was nice to dream.

When Rory spied the daily newspaper in his stack of periodicals his heart sank.

His PA left a selection of current financial newspapers and magazines on his desk, refreshing them as needed, but she steered clear of newspapers featuring gossip columns.

Unless Devlin Corp had rated a mention he'd rather avoid.

Snatching it out of the stack, he laid it flat on his desk and flipped to the middle pages, his suspicions confirmed as he spied a half-page article, complete with picture, about his dad and his latest conquest—a statuesque redhead half his age.

The article, and the number of times he spied the words *Devlin Corp* at a glance, riled him.

Rubbing his forehead, he read the article: the usual drivel about his dad flying the redhead up to the Gold Coast for a whirlwind weekend of wining and dining, speculation whether she'd be the fifth Mrs Cuthbert Devlin, and questions raised over Bert's uncanny ability to fritter away the family fortune.

Rory's fingers convulsed, bunching the newspaper, as the journalists reiterated the fall of Devlin Corp under Bert's reign, rehashing the frequent overseas jaunts on the company jet, all-nighters at the casino and a birthday bash featuring international singing sensations and chefs and French champagne, while people who'd bought homes in a Devlin Corp project were left homeless when the company stalled.

The news vultures had even brought up the Port Douglas debacle, citing some protestor's quote about the rainforest and how big developers pillaged the land.

He hated having the mistakes of his father flung in his face.

With an angry growl he balled the newspaper and lobbed it into the bin, where it belonged.

It had been six months since he'd taken over—six months during which Devlin Corp had fulfilled its obligations and clawed its way back to the top of the property game.

Reading rubbish like that in the newspaper eradicated all his hard work and that of his dedicated employees. It sucked. Why couldn't they concentrate on all Devlin Corp had achieved in the last half year? The new communities built, the new homes, the new projects on the horizon.

The company needed positive publicity, not the same old, same old, from a bunch of journalistic hacks.

His gaze fell on the scrunched newspaper in the bin as the wheels slowly turned in his head.

Positive publicity...

The hacks kept on churning out the environmental angle as often as they reported Bert's latest arm candy. What if he gave the media a more upbeat focus for their Devlin Corp mentions, affirming the company's role in protecting the environment?

No more belittling or second-guessing or implying that Devlin Corp didn't care about anything but the almighty corporate dollar. No more dubious, inconclusive, unsubstantiated implications.

What he had in mind would ensure Devlin Corp came out looking like the company most likely to sponsor Greenpeace.

Maybe it had been fortuitous Gemma Shultz had bulldozed her way into his life? He had a bona fide environmental scientist muscling in on the Portsea Point project. Why not use that to his advantage?

Having her onboard for this project would raise the profile of his business while ensuring he wouldn't face the same problems his dad had had with the eco-warriors at Port Douglas.

Win-win all round.

A definite solution to the publicity problem.

Give the newshounds something constructive rather than destructive.

Clenching his fist in a victory salute, he glanced at the digital clock on his PC screen.

Time to see how Gemma performed for the project managers and if she had what it took to be the public face for his latest campaign.

Rory joined in the light applause as Gemma's pitch concluded.

For the last half-hour he'd watched her enchant his project managers, each and every one of the hardened building professionals falling under her enthusiastic and passionate spell.

The guys were putty in her hands, and as they vied for her attention on the pretext of asking questions he sat back, folded his arms, and studied her.

She'd pulled her hair back into a low ponytail today, every strand slicked into place, and the severity of the style accentuated her heart-shaped face and large blue eyes.

She wore no make-up bar a slick of lipgloss he'd hazard to guess had more to do with keeping her lips moist than any reverence to fashion. Her simple tan shift top skimmed to mid-thigh over matching trousers. An unremarkable outfit on a remarkable body. Not that he could see much of it in the drab get-up, but he'd felt it. The way her curves had pressed against him was burned into his memory.

He didn't like his gut twisting with unexpected need, so he focussed on another pair of ridiculous earrings—

orange starfish surrounded by a silver circle—taking the marine theme to extremes.

As she elaborated on costing for solar panels as an electricity source for all housing on the Portsea project, he pondered if she'd be right for the job he had in mind.

He wanted positive PR for Devlin Corp. But depending on Gemma to put a positive spin on his latest project…? Her commitment was undoubted, but no amount of prep work could ensure success.

Rory had aced everything he touched—from high school exams to his master's degree in economics. Not from any luck the universe had bestowed on him, but through sheer hard work and determination.

Nothing beat him. Ever. His grandfather said it was because his mum was an artist with her head in the clouds and his dad couldn't concentrate on anything for longer than five seconds, so he strove to be nothing like them.

Not a bad assumption. How his flaky parents had managed to connect longer than a minute to conceive him was unfathomable.

They'd split when he was young—his mum flitting to some hippy arty commune in California, his dad bedding every female within a hundred-mile radius.

Bert had the attention span of a hyperactive-gnat in both his personal and professional lives, but his generosity and conviviality and his zest for life made him lovable.

He tolerated his dad for those qualities, loved him in his own way, but the fact that Bert had nearly driven Devlin Corp into the ground only cemented what he already knew: rely on no one, trust no one. If he wanted a job done, best to roll up his sleeves and get it done.

Relying on someone else left him feeling strangely uncertain—a foreign feeling that didn't sit well with him.

'What do you think, Rory?'

He blinked like an owl awakening, embarrassed at being figuratively caught napping. Every occupant at the boardroom table stared at him, expecting an answer, while Gemma's disappointment slapped him across the face.

She thought he hadn't been listening. Way to go with getting her onside.

'I think the idea to have a marine conservation area as part of the community is an interesting one, but I'll have to ponder further. Time we adjourned.'

He stood and strode to the front of the room, placing a hand in the small of her back, noticing her slight stiffening.

'I'd like to thank Miss Shultz for her presentation today. It was enlightening.'

She straightened her shoulders at his praise and he lowered his voice. 'Wait in my office. I'll chat with the guys and you'll have a decision shortly.'

'You're considering this?'

If her eyebrows shot any higher they'd reach her hairline.

Touched by this rare show of vulnerability, he nodded. 'Great presentation. One of the best I've seen. The energy efficiency stuff sounds feasible, the marine proposal more complicated—but, yeah, I'm considering it.'

Her eyes sparkled with enthusiasm, and before he risked having her fling her arms around him in front of the team he gave her a gentle nudge in the direction of the door.

'I'm not making promises, because the team has to vote—'

'Cut the spiel. You're the boss. You get the deciding vote and we both know it.'

Amazed at her boldness, he nudged her again. 'Go wait for me.'

With a brisk nod, she picked up her portfolio and waved to the team. Before she took a step, she murmured under her breath, 'Just for the record, I wait for no man.'

'You'll wait for *me*.'

A spark in her eyes flared at his cockiness. He didn't care. He had to get the last word in, had to establish control after her über-professional presentation had left him nonplussed.

She strode for the door; he watched—along with ten pairs of wistful eyes. The married guys were wishing they weren't, the single guys were wishing they had a shot.

Like him.

Startled by the unwelcome thought, he moved to the front of the conference room. The faster he wrapped things up, the faster he could instigate the first stage of his PR plan.

Gemma paced the office, her toes cramping in the stupid high-heeled pumps she'd worn for the occasion. How women wore these torture devices she'd never know. Give her a pair of hiking boots any day.

She was playing a part today and the shoes were an essential item in her ensemble: the professional marine environmental scientist businesswoman, who knew her stuff, who could deliver on promises.

The project guys had eaten it up, but the one man she'd had to convince had appeared unmoved during the presentation.

Rory Devlin was one cool customer and she hated not being able to read him.

She'd tried, surreptitiously watching him while she extrapolated her data to the project managers. But his face had remained an impassive mask and to her horror he'd zoned out during question time.

Not good.

Whichever way the vote went, the moment he stepped into this office she'd have to give the pitch of her life to ensure her dad's legacy was well looked after.

This was it. Last ditch stand.

If she failed she'd have to pack up and ship out. Something she'd done many times over the years. It never fazed her, yet somehow this time the thought of leaving so soon after she'd arrived left her surprisingly morose.

Living out of a suitcase, moving from job site to job site, didn't bother her—but being back in Melbourne had triggered an emotional reaction she hadn't banked on.

It had to be the loss of the land. No matter how far and wide she travelled, she'd always had Portsea to come home to, secure in the knowledge it would always be there. The one place she could be herself, cosseted by fond memories and a feeling of belonging she never had elsewhere.

Losing that felt like losing a piece of her soul, and this unusual sentimentality had her more rattled than she cared to admit.

That was the moment Mr Conservative chose to stride into his office, impressive in his black pinstripe suit, white shirt and aubergine tie. She'd never gone for suits, but the way *he* filled one out she was sorely tempted to re-evaluate her preferences.

'You disappoint me.'

Her heart plummeted. 'How?'

'I expected you to be handcuffed to my desk at the very least.'

She managed a tight smile in relief. The fact he'd made a joke had to be a good sign.

'What's the verdict?'

He paused, his poker face driving her crazy as she shuffled her weight from foot to foot, impatience taking precedence over the annoying pinching of the infernal shoes.

When he finally looked her in the eye, she had her answer before he spoke.

'You're in.'

She let out an exalted whoop, her spontaneous happy dance, complete with hip swivel and shoulder shimmy, earning an amused lip quirk.

At least it was an improvement on flinging herself into his arms: she'd given herself a stern talking-to on that front. The memory of her *faux pas* had lingered way too long, popping into her head at inopportune moments, like last thing at night, first thing in the morning and at regular intervals throughout the day. Beyond annoying.

'On one condition.'

'Anything,' she said, buoyed by the fact he'd hired her to ensure her dad's beach was preserved in the construction phase, as well as ensuring the mansions he built were energy efficient and environmentally sound.

'Anything?'

He stepped into her personal space and her pulse took off like a rocket.

'You sure about that?'

Never one to back down from a challenge, she tilted her head to look him in the eye.

'Whatever it takes to get the job done.'

The sudden, unexpected flare of heat in his eyes caught her off guard and she eased back, only to have his hands shoot out and grip her arms.

The answering zing of electricity pinging through her body short-circuited her self-preservation mechanism— the one that warned standing this close to him, having him hold her, was tantamount to sticking her finger in a power point.

'You want to work on this project? Sell your ideas to the investors. They're the money men.'

His confident grin snatched her breath.

'Without their approval, my backing means nothing.'

Another pitch? Not a problem. She'd wowed the project managers, had convinced him. She could do this.

So why the clammy palms, fidgety fingers and tumbling tummy? Had to be his proximity. Hyper-awareness zapped between them, their bodies radiating enough heat to fuel the entire project.

She noticed small, inconsequential things—like a tiny mole beneath his left ear, a shaving nick along his jaw, an old scar near his right temple. Seeing his imperfections made him more accessible, leaving her seriously unnerved.

'I'll do it.'

She eased away and he released her, his expression inscrutable.

'Great. We leave tonight.'

'Pardon?'

'The investors are holding a golf tournament at the Sebel Heritage in the Yarra Valley. They're playing all day tomorrow, so if you want to make a pitch it'll have to be later tonight. They'll convene and give a decision tomorrow.'

'We're staying overnight?'

He nodded. 'Problem with that?'

His confident stance grated: legs apart, hands in pockets, shoulders squared. He held all the power—knew she'd have to do whatever he said if she wanted to nail this and have a say in how her dad's land was treated.

She didn't like over-confident men: their cockiness, their self-assurance that the world revolved around them. While Rory didn't come across as arrogant, he had total control over this situation and it irked, big time. Or was that because his aura of assurance made him slightly irresistible?

'No problem. E-mail me the details.' Gritting her teeth at being left no option, she forced a smile. 'What time do you want me there?'

'I'll pick you up.'

She opened her mouth to protest and he held up a hand.

'Doesn't make sense to drive down in separate cars. Surely car-pooling is more environmentally friendly?'

His mouth curved into a sardonic smile and her heart gave a strange *ka-thump*.

'Besides, you can prepare for your presentation on the way.'

Damn him for his perfectly logical, perfectly thoughtful reasons.

She didn't want to spend a few hours holed up with him in a car, didn't want to rely on him for anything. But she had to wow the investors, and honing her pitch made more sense than battling evening traffic in the decrepit rental.

His probing stare focussed on her ear, and she belatedly realised she'd been tugging on her earring. She hated showing a sign of nerves.

With a brisk nod, she hitched her portfolio under her arm.

'Okay, sounds like a plan.'

She didn't understand the triumphant glint in his eyes, and nor did she like it.

CHAPTER SIX

GEMMA didn't care that the VW backfired as she pulled into her street. She had more important things to worry about, like nailing a presentation twice in the same day.

She'd kicked some serious butt with the project managers, and had been riding high on Rory's decision until he'd added the stipulation about wowing the investors. Made sense. The money-men had to approve her proposed changes. But it didn't make it any easier.

A golf trip, he'd said, and she'd inwardly groaned. She could imagine a boys-only club where she'd be scrutinised for what she wore, how much make-up she slathered on and how her hair fell.

Nightmarish, but she'd do it, play whatever game she had to, in order to protect the Portsea land that should have been hers.

As she neared home, she saw cars worth more than her annual salary lined the driveways and kerbs around the house, which could only mean one thing: Coral was entertaining.

With a scowl, she parked halfway up the street and trudged back, her ire building with every step. Yep, the stupid shoes were still pinching, but her sour mood had more to do with the well-modulated, well-cultivated voices floating on the breeze and the clink of martini glasses than any shoes.

How many times had she hidden away during one of her mum's sojourns, or snuck out of a window to avoid the stares? There'd been plenty of those on the odd occasion when she'd been sprung, from women with their noses ten feet in the air, looking down on the scruffy tomboy, their confusion unable to crinkle their Botoxed brows as they wondered how coiffed Coral could produce an off-spring like her.

They'd never said anything, not to her face, but what had rankled more than their visible derision had been the pinching around her mum's mouth—as if she'd sucked on a lemon. Not once had Coral wrapped an arm around her and included her in the conversation, proud of her daughter no matter what clothes she wore.

No, Coral had flashed a brittle smile, sagging in relief when she left, and that had hurt more than all those snooty cows put together.

The voices grew louder as she neared the back garden and she stopped, hating how the insecurities of the past had the power to affect her now. She was a professional, head-hunted by beach authorities the world over, years away from the teenage tearaway she'd been. No way would she slink around as she'd used to. She'd walk through their snobby soiree, head held high.

Decision made, she stepped around the side of the house and walked into a wall of expensive perfumes, each as overpowering as the next, trying to outdo each other as much as their owners.

They sat around a glass-topped wrought-iron table—hat-wearing socialites in dresses worth more than her rent-a-bomb car. The buzz of gossip hung in the air, and the G&Ts were flowing as freely as the name-dropping. She took a deep breath, bracing herself for the inevitable air-kisses.

Hitching her portfolio higher under her arm, she pasted a bright smile on her face and strode forward.

The buzz faded into silence as eight pairs of eyes looked her up and down, expressions ranging from puzzled to suspicious.

'Hi, ladies,' she said, enjoying their bemusement as Coral entered the back yard holding a tray of canapés. Her expression was the best of the lot: a mixture of surprise and wariness and ill-disguised discomfort.

In that moment some of her exhilaration at this morning's success evaporated on a cloud of regret. Regret that she could never be the daughter her mum wanted, regret that they were so different, regret that the one person she wanted to share her successes with was so inaccessible.

'Would you care to join us?' Coral's brusque tone made her bristle.

'No, thanks. Wouldn't want to disrupt your private party.'

Her mum hovered, uncertain, and Gemma waved her forward. 'Go ahead. I'm going to grab a bite to eat then work on the Portsea project.'

Coral's lips compressed at the P word. 'The Portsea project?'

'I mentioned it.'

But she hadn't elaborated, considering she hadn't spoken to her mum beyond pleasantries since she'd arrived. The two of them had been doing an avoidance dance bordering on the ludicrous.

While she liked not having to make polite small talk like a stranger, a small part of her—the part that wished Santa existed—wished her mum would just welcome her with open arms.

'I've been hired as the marine environmental consultant on the luxury mansions Devlin Corp is building on Dad's land, pending final approval from the investors.'

'That's wonderful!'

Coral's exuberance stunned her. But not half as much as her mum putting down the tray of canapés to give her a swift hug.

'I'm so proud of you,' she said, before releasing her.

Gemma would have reeled back in shock without the wall behind her.

'Thanks.'

Her jaw ached from the effort not to gape at her mum's rare display of affection as she watched Coral play the perfect hostess, offering canapés and topping up drinks.

Had she imagined the last few minutes, or had her mum actually said she was proud of her? Better—embraced her in front of the blue-rinse brigade?

This was why she loved the ocean. Tides and ecosystems and shifting sands were real—much easier to understand than humans.

A low tittering filled the air as Coral waved in her direction with a smile and Gemma took that as her cue to bolt. They were talking about her, and she had no intention of being a bystander.

After an hour spent honing her presentation until she could recite it in her sleep, Gemma had no option but to consider the next part of impressing the investors: her limited wardrobe.

Cold, hard facts she could handle. A mascara wand and stilettos? No way.

She'd taken a step towards her bedroom when Coral entered the kitchen.

'Guests gone?'

Coral nodded, her shoulders drooping in weariness, and Gemma noticed the wrinkles fanning from the corners of her mum's mouth. They shocked her as much as her mum's hug and declaration had earlier, for Coral had used to spend a fortune on cosmetics to maintain her youth.

A sliver of guilt lodged in her conscience. She'd been so wrapped up in her life the last few years she'd barely paid attention to her mum on her brief visits home. Whenever they'd caught up it had been out of obligation, but while they'd never be bosom buddies something had shifted when she'd walked into that garden party and been welcomed.

'Want a drink?'

Considering the number of used empty glasses on the tray, she raised an eyebrow. Coral shrugged and topped up two glasses from the pitcher she'd brought in.

'After sitting through another of those shindigs, I need it.'

Shock number two—hearing her mum voice anything other than cultivated glee at gossiping with her cronies.

Maybe she needed that drink after all. 'Sure.'

Coral handed her a glass and raised hers. 'To my clever daughter.'

Shock number three, and Gemma couldn't resist saying something. Aiming for levity, she pointed at Coral's glass. 'How many of those have you had?'

'Not enough,' she muttered, downing half her G&T in one gulp.

Oo-kay, something was definitely wrong—but Gemma wasn't skilled at this kind of thing. She didn't know whether Coral got stuck into the gin regularly and this was the alcohol talking, or a sign of some deeper malaise.

Whatever the cause, awkward and out of her depth

didn't begin to describe how she felt having this kind of conversation.

'Is something wrong?'

Coral focussed cloudy eyes on her for a long moment before shaking her head. 'Just tired.'

There was more to it, but Gemma didn't want to delve—not when she'd be ill-equipped to handle the answers.

Desperate to change the subject, she blurted, 'I'm going away tonight.'

Coral instantly perked up. 'With who?'

'Rory Devlin.'

Coral definitely didn't do Botox, for her eyebrows shot so high her forehead resembled a Sharpei.

'He gave the go-ahead on my pitch this morning, but the investors need to have the final say and they're golfing in the Yarra Valley, so we're heading down there this evening.'

Coral clearly hadn't unglued her tongue from the roof of her mouth, for she nodded and downed the rest of her drink, but there was a glint in her eyes that made Gemma want to clarify the purpose of this trip.

'It's business.'

The glint turned into a matchmaking gleam. 'Sounds lovely.'

She hadn't seen her mum so animated in years, and she wondered if it was the gin or genuine interest in her life.

'I'm good friends with his father's second wife.'

Gemma hated gossip, but she couldn't pass up an opportunity to learn more about the guy she'd be working with.

'Second wife?'

Coral grimaced. 'Cuthbert's been married four times.'

'No way!'

Coral nodded. 'I know—unbelievable. He's had about the same number of facelifts and has been between wives for a year now, so his exploits are frequently fodder for the gossip columns.'

Poor Rory. Coral might be set in her ways but at least her life wasn't plastered in the tabloids, embarrassing her kids.

'Rory seems a pretty staid guy.'

'Ethel says he's nothing like his father. In fact, he's taken over the reins of the family company after Cuthbert almost ran it into the ground.'

Ah… So that was why he was so business-focussed. She couldn't blame him there. If Devlin Corp was his family legacy he'd be fighting tooth and nail to save it— as she would have fought if she'd known her father's land was being sold off.

As much as she'd have liked to interrogate her mum again as to why she needed the money, she craved information on Rory more.

'Is Ethel Rory's mum?'

'Lord, no.'

Coral's laugh, devoid of humour, spoke volumes. 'I can't see Ethel being a mother to anyone. She married Cuthbert after Rory's mum took off when he was a youngster. The marriage lasted two years before Cuthbert moved on.'

Once again she sympathised with Rory. It had killed her to lose her dad. What must it have been like for him, losing his mother, then having to accept a stepmother only to have her move on shortly after? Not the best upbringing to build emotional attachments.

While she might not have been as close to her mum as she would have liked following her dad's death, they'd been a family when he'd been alive, and she'd been lavished with the attention and affection every kid needed to thrive.

'Funny thing is they're still the best of friends.'

'Who? Ethel and Cuthbert?'

Coral nodded. 'They frequently hit the town together. Ethel loves the high life; Cuthbert lives it.'

A shrewd gleam entered her mum's eye. A gleam she didn't like one bit.

'I could have a dinner party…invite them and—'

'Stop right there.'

Gemma held up her hands and slid off the bar stool. 'I don't need you interfering.'

The last thing she needed was her mum poking her nose into her business relationship with Rory and turning it into something it wasn't.

'I'm only trying to help.'

She'd never heard her mum's voice wobble, let alone seen her with a wounded expression, but she couldn't afford to waver on this. Before she knew it Coral would have them marching up the aisle.

'Thanks, but I can handle it.'

Coral topped up her glass and Gemma gritted her teeth to stop herself telling her to take it easy. She had no right and if she didn't want her mum interfering in her life, she had no place doing the same.

'Do you date much?'

Hell, this was what happened when she tried to bond with her mum. She faced an interrogation she'd rather avoid.

'Enough.'

'Anyone serious?'

She could bluff and throw in a few fake names, but she was proud of her choices, proud she'd built a solid,

commendable career at the expense of a meaningful relationship.

And those doubts that crept into her head late at night,
whispering that she'd end up alone if she kept pushing
guys away for fear of letting anyone too close? Not worth
worrying about—not when she felt more comfortable with
marine life than living the high life on the dating merry-
go-round.

'Not really.' This time *she* reached for the pitcher.
'Work keeps me busy and I move around a lot.'

Coral stared at her over the rim of her glass, her eyes
huge and filled with worry. 'What about starting a family of your own one day—'

That was her cue to leave. She downed the G&T in two
gulps and grabbed her laptop, wishing she'd never mentioned raising kids as an argument to flay Coral with for
selling her dad's land.

'I appreciate your concern, Mum, but I'm fine. I'm
going away with Rory on *business.* So don't over-analyse
anything or feel sorry for me, because I like my life just
the way it is.'

'Okay.'

Coral's easy capitulation raised her suspicions, but she
couldn't see anything beyond an aggravating pity in her
eyes before she lowered them to concentrate on her drink.

'I need to get ready.'

'Would you like some help?'

If the impromptu chat she'd had with her mother hadn't
bamboozled her enough, Coral's invitation to help her get
ready sent her into a tailspin.

She'd rarely dated as a teenager—guys had tended to
be intimidated by her ability to kick the football further,
score more points in basketball and swim the fastest and

furthest in any race—so they'd never done the mother/daughter tizzy stuff. Surely it was too late to start now?

Then she made the fatal mistake of glancing at her mum. Her hopeful expression combined with her trembling hand as she twirled the glass undermined her instant refusal.

'I could do your hair? Lend you this incredible new mineral make-up that looks like you're not wearing any?'

She'd never seen Coral anything other than poised and elegant and confident, even after her dad's death, and the fact her mum was practically begging to help went some way to breaching the yawning emotional gap between them.

Besides, in the dress-to-impress department she needed all the help she could get.

'Okay.'

Coral's tremulous smile made her feel something she hadn't in a long time when it came to her mum: hope. Maybe it wasn't too late to bridge the distance between them after all this time?

'You go up. I'll finish stacking the dishwasher and be up to give you a hand shortly.'

Feeling more light-hearted than she had in years, Gemma took the stairs two at a time, the fizz in her veins lending an extra spring to her step.

Had to be the gin, and nothing at all to do with the tentative overtures of her mum or the prospect of spending the night in the company of one seriously hot guy—albeit for business.

That was her excuse and she was sticking to it.

'What on earth is all that?'

Gemma took one look at the paraphernalia in her

mum's arms and stepped back, instantly regretting her acceptance of Coral's offer to help her get ready.

Moving faster than Gemma had seen in years, Coral dumped her booty onto the bed and rubbed her hands together.

'Hair straightener. Curling tongs. Epilator. Eyelash curler. Make-up brush set. Light mirror.'

Gemma shook her head, not encouraged by her mum's determined smile.

'I was going to wear my hair in a ponytail, so I don't need all that hair stuff.' She batted her eyelashes. 'That curler? Redundant. Nothing could curl these straight pokers.' Puffing out her cheeks, noting their pallor, she exhaled. 'The make-up? Couldn't hurt.'

Coral picked up a small square device with a bristly steel head. 'What about the epilator?'

'That depends. What does it do?'

'Hair removal.'

Coral's glance dipped to her legs as realisation hit: her mum thought she might need to de-fuzz. Which meant her mum also thought there was a fair chance her legs would be bared tonight.

Dying from embarrassment, she held up her hands. Yeah—as if *that* would ward off an incoming beauty expert hell-bent on making her over.

'Let's stick to the make-up.'

Coral swapped the epilator for one of the hair thingies. 'And the hair. Nothing like sleek hair to glam up.'

'I don't do glam,' she muttered, but her protest fell on deaf ears as her mum urged her to sit on the stool in front of the mirror while she bustled around, plugging in the straightener, unfolding her satchel of brushes, laying out make-up on the dresser.

As she glanced at her bare face in the mirror, at the

frizzy blond strands spiking out of her loose plait, she couldn't help but be thankful she'd accepted her mum's offer.

She might be confident in her abilities, but she'd be lying if she didn't admit to being the teensiest bit intimidated at the thought of standing up in a room full of suited-up guys who'd probably pick her proposal apart.

She'd be judged on appearances too, and presenting a confident front would work wonders. She'd nail this pitch if it killed her.

She loved a challenge—always had. Land the biggest fish of the day? She wouldn't move off the pier until she'd caught it. Swim in the freezing ocean on a winter's day? She'd be first off the boat and ride the boom-net the longest. See the first Bottlenose dolphin of the season? She'd don wetsuit and fins every day, waiting for a glimpse of her beloved creatures.

Have a super-confident, commanding millionaire in control, thinking she'd quiver in her work boots in front of a roomful of his high-flying cronies?

Bring it on.

'Ready?'

Coral hovered over her and Gemma nodded, trying not to stiffen when her mum tugged the elastic off the end of her plait and unravelled it with her fingers.

How old had she been when she'd last submitted to having her hair done? Eight? Nine? It was one of the few girly things she remembered truly enjoying as a kid, having her mum brush her hair every morning and night with strong, smooth strokes that lulled.

'You've always had such lovely healthy hair,' Coral said, picking up a brush and running it from her scalp to the ends in the same reassuring way she'd done as a child.

'Thanks,' Gemma said, the word squeezing past the

unexpected lump in her throat, and when their gazes met in the mirror she knew Coral understood her gratitude was for more than brushing her hair.

In a way, she hadn't only lost her dad when he'd died. She'd lost her mum too. She'd put it down to mourning at the time, both of them withdrawing into their private worlds to cope. But later, when the initial horror had faded, replaced by an insidious sadness invading on a daily basis, she'd needed her mum. Had needed comforting and hugs and reassurance.

She hadn't got it. They'd been so consumed by their initial grief that once it eased they were different people, virtual strangers, and neither knew how to reach out to the other.

The lump in her throat grew as Coral gently ran thick strands of her hair through the heated straightener, a small satisfied smile curving her lips as she bit down on the tip of her tongue in concentration.

How could something so simple bring so much satisfaction to her mum?

'There. All done.'

As Coral ran her palms over her shiny hair, hanging like a sleek curtain past her shoulders, their gazes caught in the mirror again and Gemma had her answer.

Her mum's eyes were filled with hope and yearning, and the sheen of tears accentuated what she'd already suspected. Offering to help her prep for her presentation meant more than the grooming and appearances Coral valued.

This had been an olive branch.

When she tried a tentative, grateful smile, and watched her mum's expression transform into one of joy, she knew she'd done the right thing.

Interrogating her about the land could wait.

CHAPTER SEVEN

Rory had always been upstanding, always played by the rules, always played fair.

Hiring Gemma for her profile more than her expertise niggled, but after seeing Devlin Corp besmirched yet again in the papers, courtesy of dear old dad, he had to do something.

Not that his plan was all *that* nefarious. Gemma's presentation had genuinely impressed him, and he could see the viability of her proposal. But he'd orchestrated the meeting with his investors with one goal in mind.

To have her front and centre as the environmental face of the Portsea Point construction.

The investors had already received a memo from him this afternoon, outlining why hiring her was a viable proposition.

They'd been amenable to seeing her presentation, and from early feedback he'd received via e-mail she'd have to botch it for them not to go for it.

Not that he'd told her any of this. He wanted to see her pull out all stops, wanted her to prove herself—if for no other reason than to cement this decision as a purely business one, and eradicate the constant nagging feeling that he wasn't averse to having her stick around for a while.

He'd been distracted at work all afternoon, thinking

about her unusual qualities and why she piqued his interest when she was nothing like the women in his sphere. No smoothness, no polish, no artifice; she intrigued and terrified him.

He didn't like surprises as a rule. He'd had a gutful of them growing up, whenever Bert had brought home his latest conquest and introduced her as yet another step-mum-to-be. Those vacuous, self-absorbed usurpers who'd seen his dad as an easy meal-ticket and had sucked up to him because they'd thought it would curry favour with the old man.

He'd hated every moment of it and had grown immune to them, relying on practised indifference to get him through.

Surprises sucked. Yet Gemma Shultz had been one big surprise wrapped up in a very attractive package since he'd met her.

Who knew? Maybe some surprises weren't so bad after all?

As he strode up the manicured path towards her front door she slipped out, hoisting a small, scruffy backpack that had seen its fair share of travel, and quickly shut the door.

He raised his hand in greeting, immediately regretting the dorkish gesture. The whisky he'd consumed at work with his deputy burned in his belly, spreading its heat outwards, making him sweat, and he surreptitiously slid a finger between his tie and collar.

He couldn't breathe. The air was sucked out of his lungs as she strolled towards him. He was confounded by his reaction to this extraordinary woman.

'I knew you'd bring your fancy car.' She jerked her thumb towards the Merc.

'Better than squeezing into that.' He pointed at the

rusty rental and she nodded, toying with an earring—a black seal in spun gold this time.

'It's not so bad.'

He'd rarely seen her anything other than bold and sassy, so her flash of uncertainty as she glanced at the run-down car made him want to haul her in for a comforting hug.

'You look great, by the way.'

'Really?'

Her fingers tugged at the end of her flowing peasant top, smoothed the sides of her denim skirt, and her nervousness struck him again.

'Yeah, really.'

His gaze skimmed her glossy hair, shimmering like the sun. Her eyes were accentuated by subtle cosmetics, making them appear glistening and seductive.

His gut wrenched. He liked it better when she stuck to ugly suits, ponytails and no make-up.

Her eyes widened, as if she'd read his thoughts. 'I've got my suit in here.' She tapped the backpack. 'Benefits of non-crushable fabric and travelling light.'

'Your room should be ready, so you'll have plenty of time to change once we check in.'

Considering the way his mind had taken a detour from the business at hand, he felt the need to state the obvious—separate rooms—if only for his benefit.

'Good to know.'

Her mouth quirked into a playful smile, socking him like a jab to the jaw.

'Just in case I had the wrong idea.'

Her soft laughter taunted and, unable to rein in the insane impulse to touch her, he reached out and slid his palm over her hair, shiny and sleek, framing her expertly made-up face like a stunning backdrop.

It trailed through his fingertips like silk, tantalisingly

soft, and he bit back a groan when his bemused gaze clashed with hers.

He had no idea if her eyes held promise or if his imagination was working overtime, but whatever the hell was going on here he had as much control over it as he did over his father: absolutely none.

Her tongue flicked out to moisten her bottom lip and his fingers convulsed.

Screw propriety. Screw appearances.

He'd spent a lifetime doing the right thing, trying to be the opposite of his dad, but in that second he'd never wanted to kiss a woman more.

So he did.

He leaned forward and placed a kiss just shy of her glossed mouth, lingering longer than he should, but not giving a damn. The way he was feeling—reckless and floundering—she was lucky he didn't go for the lips.

He stiffened when she smiled against his mouth and eased away.

'If you're trying to distract me in the hope I'll botch the presentation and you'll be rid of me, think again.'

Her teasing smile slugged him in the chest. Time to back-pedal. Fast.

'We're going to be late.'

He picked up her backpack, wishing he'd never offered to pick her up, wishing he'd never kissed her. He hated his abrupt tone, hated the laughter in her eyes chastising him for being a stuffy fool, but if he didn't get behind the wheel right now and concentrate on the road who knew what he'd end up doing?

'Wouldn't want that.'

He ignored her smirk, mentally chastising himself for being a fool and unnecessarily complicating matters.

It wasn't until they'd hit the freeway that Rory realised

he hadn't given the Portsea project a second thought once Gemma had strutted out through her front door.

The moment Rory drove through the Sebel Heritage front gate and along its long, winding, tree-lined drive Gemma was catapulted back to her teens.

Arriving at a party to find the girls decked out in make-up and dresses while she wore jeans and her best T-shirt.

Walking into class to find her classmates discussing manicures while she wanted to chat about the weekend footy scores.

Coming downstairs every day to find her mother immaculately made-up, no matter what the hour, while she slouched around in whatever shorts were clean.

She'd never fitted in.

Since her teens she'd been the odd one out, and while she'd grown to value her individuality as she got older entering *this* exclusive enclave resurrected her old doubts like nothing else.

As if she wasn't nervous enough already. She'd agreed to pitch tonight. She hadn't agreed on kissing Rory Devlin.

'We're here.'

'Great.' She managed a tight smile as he meandered along the never-ending driveway, looking but not seeing the designer townhouses lining the fairways, the Heritage Retreat and Mii Spa, the sprawling clubhouse.

If driving into this place hadn't rattled her enough, his kiss had done it. The way he'd touched her hair, along with his genuine compliment, had made her feel special and desirable and feminine. As she'd mulled over his motivation for the entire two-hour drive, while pretending to hone her presentation, she'd come to the startling conclusion that she could end up feeling more for this guy than was good for her.

He pulled up under an elaborate portico, increasing her foreboding.

She didn't belong in a place like this.

It might be for only one night, and on business, but staying in an exclusive resort raised her hackles. She'd rather be roughing it in a tent than holed up in some posh hotel room, trying not to climb the walls.

She might have been raised in an upper-class suburb and attended a private school but she'd been an outcast, and being surrounded by obvious wealth disconcerted her, reminding her of every instance when she hadn't belonged growing up.

It was why Portsea meant so much—why losing the land had ripped a hole in her carefully constructed confidence. Having a safe place to go to, *her* place, where she could be herself, had meant the world to a tough girl determined on hiding her vulnerabilities. Take that away and she risked stripping down the rest of her defences too. Scary.

Clamping down on the urge to balk and stay in the car, she entered the cosy foyer alongside Rory, trying not to stare at her dishevelled backpack next to his designer overnight bag.

The faded denim backpack had frayed straps, a broken zip on the front pocket, and a tiny hole in the bottom left corner. Next to his bag, with the designer's shiny logo embossing it, it looked tacky, reinforcing the yawning gap between them.

She was natural, earthy, without pretence.

He was smooth, slick, without a clue as to what made someone like her tick.

So why the hell couldn't she forget that kiss?

'Here's your keycard.'

He handed her a small folder and she tried not to

snatch it so she could bolt for the sanctuary of her room. 'Thanks.'

'We're next to each other.'

Goody.

'The presentation's at eight?'

He nodded, his probing stare making her uncomfortable. Not that she blamed him for trying to fathom why she'd switched from enthusiastic to withdrawn.

'There's a conference room next to the Lodge Bar.' He snapped his keycard against his palm repeatedly, on edge. 'I can make a dinner reservation at the Bella if you like—'

'Thanks, but I couldn't possibly eat anything before the presentation. I'll grab some room service later.'

'No worries.'

But there were plenty of worries, judging by the awkward, stilted conversation. She'd gone from having the upper hand, savouring her power to unsettle this uptight businessman, to perpetually remembering how he'd loosened up long enough to kiss her.

'We better head up to our room…s,' he said, his slip lightening the tension, making her chuckle while he ducked his head to grab the bags.

'Let's do that,' she said, back to her confident best as she shot him a coy smile.

His lips thinned as he shouldered the bags and strode ahead, as fast as his long legs could carry him.

After a sleepless night, Rory rolled out of bed at 6:00 a.m., punching his pillow in frustration along the way.

How on earth had Gemma messed with his head in twenty-four hours? If she'd impressed him during her pitch to the project managers yesterday morning, her presentation to the investors last night had blown him away.

He knew the investors had been sold, even though they'd made a grand show of deliberating and making them wait for a final decision until after their early-morning golf game today.

He should be rapt. His plan to use her as the face of Portsea Point would come to fruition.

If he didn't go insane in the process.

He'd sat through a full hour of her presentation, using the sixty minutes to mentally list every reason he shouldn't be attracted to her.

Nothing in common; complete opposites; eco-obsessed versus city-savvy; batty scientist versus levelheaded businessman.

When he'd still found himself staring at her legs and working his way up he'd started nit-picking, adding average fashion sense and atrocious taste in jewellery and awful shoes to his list.

Only to find himself counteracting each and every one of his petty arguments by noticing the way her nose crinkled when she was really concentrating, how she smiled with her eyes as well as her mouth, how she lit up a room by being in it.

He didn't want to be attracted to her—didn't want to complicate their business arrangement. But no way would he let Devlin Corp suffer if he made bad decisions from lack of sleep.

He confronted issues head-on.

He'd do the same with Gemma.

Starting today.

'You don't strike me as the picnic type.'

Gemma stifled a grin as Rory tightened his grip on the picnic basket. She shouldn't bait him, she really shouldn't, but who went on a picnic wearing a suit?

'We need to wait for the investors to make their final decision—better to wait outside than in.'

A logical explanation—she'd expect nothing less from him—but she couldn't shake the feeling there was more behind his impromptu invitation.

'True.'

While breakfast at the Bella Restaurant had been superb, she'd been too fidgety to enjoy the amazing Bircher muesli and delicious crêpes.

She'd been hyped-up after her presentation last night, hadn't slept, and the adrenalin hadn't subsided this morning. That was her excuse for placing her palm flat against the wall next to her bed, wistfully imagining Rory doing the same on the other side.

Unbelievable. For a woman without a romantic bone in her body she'd done a good job of romanticising that brief greeting kiss. All night.

At least she'd been smart enough not to tempt fate and had bolted after the presentation finished. The last thing she'd needed was to sit around with Rory in a cosy bar downing drinks.

If he'd seemed distracted during her morning pitch, he'd been one hundred percent focussed last night—to the point she'd almost squirmed under his intense scrutiny.

At one stage his stare had been so potent, so mesmerising, she would have sworn he could see right down to her soul.

She'd soldiered on, pretending she was talking to a roomful of blobby jellyfish—her technique for being at ease during public speaking—not risking another glance his way.

It had worked, and she'd been suitably confident she'd nailed her presentation. She wished she could be as confident of handling Rory and his strange mood this morning.

'How's this spot?'

They'd strolled along the walking trail on the periphery of the hotel for ten minutes before he'd stopped on the banks of the Yarra River.

'Perfect.'

He produced a purple picnic blanket from the basket, spreading it like an amethyst cape on a field of emerald.

She slipped off her sandals and stared pointedly at his shoes. He looked at her feet, his, and frowned.

'Come on—you're not seriously having a riverside picnic wearing shoes?'

'I guess not,' he muttered, slipping off his shoes and stuffing his socks into them.

He had sexy feet, she thought, belatedly realising she was staring when he wriggled his toes.

She sighed as her feet hit dirt, savouring the warm grittiness on her soles. She loved the gravel texture under her feet almost as much as she loved the grating of sand.

No matter how many beaches she visited around the world, when she first dug her toes into the sand it always felt like coming home.

Her dad had sworn the only reason she'd got good grades at school was because she'd lived for their weekends at the beach. He'd been right. She'd always finished her work in class, because homework meant time away from the outdoors after school and homework on the weekends meant no Portsea.

She'd loved those weekends. Loved the ocean spray in her face and the sand between her toes and the icy brace of the sea. Loved swimming and building sandcastles and playing beach cricket.

Mum would set up the umbrella and lay out lemonade

and peanut butter sandwiches on the towels before settling back to read, while she cavorted with her dad. They'd
been happy—a close family unit. She'd missed that famil-
ial bond after her dad died as much as she'd missed him.

Thinking of her dad and how her relationship with her
mum had been fractured always made her melancholy,
and she wished she hadn't headed down memory lane.

No beach came close to what Portsea meant to her and
never would. The thought that some rich folk who probably wouldn't appreciate it would be living on her land in
their fancy mansions… Best not go there. No use spoiling
this picnic before it had begun.

'Great spot.'

He nodded and sat next to her, knees bent, forearms
resting on top of them, as he stared out over the sludgy
Yarra.

She mirrored him, content to stare at the water and
feel the warmth of his deliciously close body radiating
towards her.

She never felt completely comfortable around guys like
Rory: rich, powerful, able to command attention with a
wave of their pinkie. She'd worked with enough of them
to know.

Yet sitting here with Rory seemed different. *He* was
different, with a heart of gold underlying his steely exterior.

Despite her unusual tactics, he hadn't had to grant her
an interview. And he certainly hadn't had to give her an
opportunity to pitch her ideas to his project team or the
investors while footing the bill.

People usually did things for a reason, were motivated
by all sorts of causes from money to recognition and everything in between. She'd like to think Rory wasn't like
that, but how well did she really know him?

A corporate go-getter like him wouldn't cave easily to demands, yet he'd given her a chance when she'd expected she'd need to browbeat him. More than that, he understood her rationale and seemingly supported her environmental quest. The sad thing was, she wondered why.

This picnic only served to heighten her suspicions. She never let people close for a reason: if even her mother rejected the real her, why was a busy businessman taking time out? And why was he being so darn nice to her?

She didn't like her defences crumbling and that was what was happening. With every smile, with every nicety, he was slowly chipping away at the emotional armour she'd been developing since the first time she'd realised her uniqueness wasn't always appreciated. So she went in for the kill.

'Why did you kiss me yesterday?'

He didn't answer, his forehead creased in thought. When he finally looked at her, the confusion in his eyes mirrored hers.

'I have no idea.'

She snorted. 'That's a cop-out.'

He rubbed the back of his neck, out of his comfort zone. 'You're not like any woman I've met before.'

'Good to know.'

He winced, as if her sense of humour pained him as much as his momentary slip in kissing her.

'I don't want you to get the wrong idea.' His nose crinkled, as if the river had washed up rank reeds. 'I don't do complications and drama and the inevitable fallout of getting involved.'

She should have been pleased he was a fellow relationship cynic, but his answer disappointed her somehow.

'Then why do it?'

He plucked at blades of grass, tossing them in the air,

watching them fall, buying time before reluctantly meeting her curious gaze.

'Because you intrigue me. You bowled me over the way you barged your way into an interview with gumption and sass. But most of all because I really want to do this.'

He captured her face in his hands and lowered his lips to hers, brushing them once, twice, before giving in to the irresistible pull between them and kissing her. A deep, hot, luscious kiss that lasted for ever and left her leaning all over him—because she didn't have a hope of sitting up straight with her boneless spine.

'Wow.'

She touched her lips and his gaze darkened.

'Wow is the effect you have on me.'

Their stunned gazes held for five long, loaded seconds before she glanced away, her heart pounding in exhilaration, her head throbbing with confusion.

Having Rory kiss her might set her on fire physically, but logically it didn't make any sense.

She didn't want to like him.

He was the enemy—a money-oriented, autocratic property developer who defiled the environment she loved.

On the flipside, he'd demonstrated an unexpected spontaneity by organising this picnic, and an admirable honesty in professing confusion over his rationale for kissing her.

She confused him? The feeling was entirely mutual.

'You hungry?'

'Ravenous.'

He wasn't looking at the hamper.

Before she straddled him and cut loose, she flipped open the basket on the pretext of looking at the food.

The hotel had done well, and her stomach rumbled

as she helped set out salmon and asparagus rolls, figs wrapped in prosciutto, crusty baguettes slathered in duck and walnut pâté, cheese scones with caramelised onion jam, brie quiche and tropical fruit skewers.

When she pulled out a bottle of Shiraz, she studied the label in surprise. 'Great drop. My dad had this vintage in his cellar.'

She handed it to him for the uncorking honours.

'You know this is on a par with Grange Hermitage, right?'

'In that case I'm surprised Mum didn't sell that too,' she muttered, wishing Coral had flogged the wine before the land.

'Her selling the land must've really divided you.'

She didn't want to discuss this, not with him, but it was the lesser of two evils.

Talk about her mother or dwell on that kiss? Considering her heart rate hadn't slowed and her lips still tingled, no contest.

'We were already divided.' She picked at the edges of the wine label until it frayed. 'After Dad died we drifted apart and nothing I did seemed good enough.'

He raised an eyebrow. 'You must've had decent grades to get into science at uni?'

'Academically I wasn't a problem.'

She laid the bottle down, half its label stripped. 'I was a tomboy and our interests never matched. We co-existed in the same house but were worlds apart. It felt like…'

Heck, why had she opened up? He didn't want to join a pity-party any more than she did.

'Like what?'

Balling her hands, she willed the sting of tears away.

'Like she couldn't accept me for who I was so she rejected me instead.'

She focussed on a far tree-line, waiting for the blur in her eyes to clear.

'I'm sorry.'

He touched her shoulder and she struggled not to flinch.

'Don't be. I learned a long time ago to depend on no one.'

'Me too.' He squeezed her shoulder and released it. 'Not sure what's worse. Having a mum emotionally shut down or not having a mum at all.'

She knew via the Coral gossip grapevine his mum had left, but she couldn't let on—not without giving away the fact she'd been discussing him.

'What happened with yours?'

He shrugged, his expression impassive. She'd bet he'd spent a lifetime honing it, as she had.

'She was an artist, pretty flighty. Couldn't tolerate Dad's infidelities—not that I blame her—so she left when I was five.'

'That's so young.'

'Yeah, I missed her at the start.'

'Did your dad step up?'

He snorted. 'My dad stepped *out*. Continually. But at least he hung around and didn't ship me off somewhere, so it's all good.'

'Do you hear from your mum?'

The tightness around his mouth softened as he nodded. 'All the time. We e-mail, Skype, chat on the phone. She's the same scatterbrain, wrapped up in her pastels and oils, oblivious to reality. But she stays in touch—guess that's the main thing.'

She envied him. He was a guy whose parents seemed flaky at best, but he'd come to terms with it. Shame she couldn't say the same for herself.

Sadness clogged her throat, and she grabbed a glass from Rory's outstretched hand and took several sips of the exquisite wine.

'Easy.' A worry line had appeared between his brows. 'How about we forget our dysfunctional families and enjoy the picnic?'

Annoyed she'd become maudlin—though it had succeeded in distracting her from that kiss—she smiled and gestured at the food.

'Let's eat.'

Gemma glanced at her empty driveway and breathed a sigh of relief. Her mum wasn't home so there was no risk of her interrogating Rory and embarrassing her.

'Would you like to come in?'

She issued the invitation out of politeness, hoping he'd refuse. The last thing she wanted was to spend more time with him after blurting out her innermost fears during that picnic.

Thankfully, apart from that hiccup, it had been a success. They'd eaten—or he'd eaten. She'd toyed with a cheese scone, her appetite lost along with all common sense when she'd divulged her private thoughts—and they'd talked. They'd shared an impulsive hug when the investors had rung through their decision.

She had the job.

They'd headed back to the clubhouse and shared a drink with a few of the guys post-game at the Nicklaus Bar, but their back-slapping camaraderie had reeked of old boys' club exclusivity and she'd been relieved when Rory had indicated it was time to leave.

There'd been no buffer of her work on the ride home, and she'd been forced to chat and smile and pretend as if nothing had happened between them at the Sebel: the kiss, the shared family tales, the inevitable bonding.

It had been the longest drive of her life.

'Do you make a wicked espresso?'

His adorable smile made her heart leap—she couldn't do this, couldn't risk blurring the lines further.

She'd already revealed too much, had allowed him to get closer than any guy ever had. The faster she slammed her defences back in place, the happier she'd be.

'Sorry, instant's all I've got on offer.'

His smile faded at her abruptness. 'Thanks. Maybe another time?'

'Sure.'

She heard the disappointment in his glib reply. She'd bet it wasn't a patch on hers. 'I e-mailed the project manager from the car. We're meeting on-site tomorrow. Will you be there?'

'Not sure. Back-to-back meetings all day.'

'See you next week, then.'

He frowned, staring at her, trying to convey some silent message she had no hope of interpreting.

'Come down with me Saturday,' he blurted, folding and unfolding his shirt cuff. 'I'd planned on heading down for the day, and we can get a lot of work done without tradesmen buzzing around.'

Her heart leapt at his initial invitation before reality slapped it down. Of *course* he'd join her on the Peninsula for work. What did she expect? After one picnic he'd be romancing her?

While he'd been attentive and chivalrous, he couldn't have stated his intentions any plainer: he didn't do involvement. What had he said? Something about no dramas and complications?

Normally she would have agreed with him, but then

he'd kissed her…and what a kiss. A kiss to remember, a kiss to resurrect on lonely evenings, a kiss to build foolish dreams on if she was that way inclined. She wasn't. Thank goodness.

'Getting a jump start on work sounds good.'

His brisk nod was a world away from the passionate way he'd kissed her next to the river, and her resident imp couldn't resist pinching his propriety.

'It'll be fun.'

'Fun?' he parroted, as if he couldn't quite comprehend the meaning of the word.

She laughed. 'Yeah, fun. I love Portsea Beach, so working on my passion—it'll be great.'

She accentuated *passion,* drew the word out, vindicated when his Adam's apple bobbed as he swallowed.

'Yeah, great.'

He flung open the door so fast he almost tumbled out. She opened hers.

'Rory?'

'Yeah?'

He ducked his head, but not far enough, and it clunked against the doorframe. She winced but he didn't react, his gaze fixed on her.

'Thanks.'

For giving her this work opportunity, for being so understanding, for telling her he'd see her on Saturday albeit for work.

'No worries.'

He straightened and she stepped out, snagging her backpack from the foot well.

'Now, go—before—'

'Before what?'

Before I blurt any more deep, dark secrets.

Before I re-evaluate my stance to reassemble my tat-tered emotional defences against you.

Before I forget every logical reason why I shouldn't like you and fall for you regardless.

A myriad of emotions flitted across his face and she focussed on the desire darkening his eyes to indigo.

'Before I turn into a pumpkin.'

Lame by any standards. His slight grimace made her laugh.

'See you Saturday.'

He headed towards the driver's door, not breaking eye contact until he'd slid into the car.

When he gunned away, and her heart roared in response, she deliberately walked towards the house without a backward glance.

CHAPTER EIGHT

IT HAD BEEN a while since Gemma had pulled an all-nighter, and as she rolled out of bed she blinked at the alarm clock. Her gritty eyes and stuffy head were testament to three hours' broken sleep, and she yawned, did a few yoga poses, and tried to figure out if she'd dreamt yesterday.

Rory's candid admission that she intrigued him, the impromptu picnic, the shared confidences, the kiss.

In the grand scheme of things it meant little, and she wanted it that way, but during those sleepless hours she'd imagined what it would be like to be involved with a guy like him.

Not the usual dating merry-go-round she rode, content not to have demands placed on her, but *really* involved: mentally, physically, emotionally. Equals in every way it counted.

Stupid, because they were poles apart, but a girl could dream, right? That kiss had been the catalyst for her fruitless fantasies.

He should never have done it.

She should never have let him.

It had blurred the edges of their relationship, taking it beyond business, tempting her to be take a risk and show him exactly how intriguing she could be.

His supreme confidence brought out the worst in her, prompting her to tease a reaction out of him. Maybe she'd invited the kiss? In which case, note to self: *stop taunting him, unless you want more.*

She'd analysed it at great length last night when she couldn't sleep. Her practical side said she must be different from every woman he'd ever dated so he'd been tempted to explore why. Her wistful side, the side she hadn't known existed until *the kiss,* basked in the unexpected power she could exert over a commanding guy like him.

Thankfully, practicality won out. He'd gotten too close yesterday, creeping under the barriers she'd erected many years ago out of necessity, tempting her to trust.

She'd never spoken of her mother to anyone, had never articulated her fears of rejection and not being good enough. Deep, personal fears she barely acknowledged let alone divulged to a virtual stranger.

Rory had a way about him, a way of crawling under her guard and getting her to believe in him, and it terrified her.

No doubt about it: she had to forget that kiss, forget her momentary lapse yesterday, forget his empathy, and focus.

Satisfied she'd clarified the situation in her own mind, she pulled on work jeans and a khaki drill shirt, slipped her feet into steel-capped boots and tied her hair into a ponytail. No fuss, no frills—exactly how she liked it.

Flipping open a small wooden box with a dolphin carved on the lid, she chose a pair of earrings—clownfish today—and threaded them through the holes in her ears. They were her one concession to frippery, and she liked having her marine friends dangling from her ears and brushing against her neck.

She'd collected the earrings all around the world, hoarding them in the special box hand-carved by her dad.

Her fingertip traced the outline of the dolphin and she smiled, remembering her adamant demands that he carve a dolphin and his indulgent smile as he'd quietly done just that.

This box had travelled with her from Jamaica to Jaipur, Mexico to Marbella, and everywhere in between. It gave her comfort, a solid link to her dad, one of many memories to treasure. Even more important now his land had been sold.

Pulling a face at the mirror, she adjusted the elastic on her ponytail. While she could do without make-up, she liked the sleek hair. Not that she'd succumb to the ritual of virtually ironing her hair every time she washed it, but having it hang past her shoulders in a shiny tail was kind of nice.

She had ten minutes to grab a piece of toast and hit the road before she ran into peak hour traffic. The project managers were meeting on-site at seven-thirty. She planned on being there first.

The light under the kitchen door surprised her, and she edged it open, stunned to see her mum cradling a steaming mug of coffee and poring over the early-edition morning papers.

'I have a reason to be up at this ungodly hour—what's yours?'

Coral glanced up from the papers, her shy smile as confusing as seeing her in a dressing gown and without make-up.

'I'm up at five every morning these days.'

'Really?'

'Becomes a habit after a while.'

When Coral didn't divulge why, Gemma popped two

slices of bread into the toaster. She didn't have time to delve into the reasons behind her mum's insomnia, and even if she did she wouldn't want to. Yesterday had been nice, a tentative start to bridging the gap between them, but she wasn't in the mood to get all deep and meaningful on a few hours' sleep.

'Have a nice time away?'

'It was business.'

And that was all she'd say on the matter. Until her mum smirked and pushed the newspaper across the table.

'Looks like Rory Devlin was impressed by your business.'

Confused, she glanced at the paper upside down. It was some features snippet between the gossip column and the horoscopes she'd never read in a million years.

Except today. Considering she was front and centre.

Coral chuckled as she snatched the paper and flipped it to read the accompanying article.

Millionaire CEO Rory Devlin is pleased to announce the addition of environmental scientist and marine specialist Gemma Shultz to the project team at Portsea Point, the latest of Devlin Corp's high-end developments.

Since taking over the reins of Devlin Corp six months ago the CEO has been busy boosting profit margins and re-establishing the business as Australia's premier luxury property developer.

Devlin Corp's exclusive enclaves have flourished along the east coast of Australia, with their signature opulent mansions built in Port Douglas, Surfers Paradise, Byron Bay, Coffs Harbour and Manly.

With Devlin Corp commencing work on a new

*lavish development in Portsea shortly, Ms Shultz's
expertise will be welcomed to maintain the ecology
along the coastline.*

    *Rory Devlin couldn't speak highly enough of
his new consultant.*

'I bet,' she muttered, shoving the paper away with one
finger.

'He must be impressed with you to give a glowing rec-
ommendation already—'

'News must be on a go-slow if that's the kind of boring stuff they're printing.'

Coral's grin widened. 'Perhaps you're irked they used
an old CV photo and not one of you with lovely sleek
hair?'

Gemma shot her a death glare. 'I'm a professional,
Mum, who spends her days on a beach. Wind. Salty air.
Think my hair's important?'

Coral filled a mug with coffee and placed it in front of
her, tweaking her ponytail. The simple action was so rem-
iniscent of her childhood that a lump lodged in Gemma's
throat.

'It pays to always look your best.'

'No one cares how I look when I'm testing E. coli levels.'

Except you. But she wisely kept that to herself. They
were getting along. No use aggravating the situation.

Coral wrinkled her nose at the mention of E. coli, and
Gemma took the opportunity to slather butter on her toast
while casting surreptitious glances at the article.

Mr Conservative couldn't speak highly enough of her,
huh? She'd never let him live this down.

When she looked up, her mum was studying her as if
she were a micro-organism under a microscope.

'You like him, don't you?'

'Mum, I'm not in high school,' she mumbled, taking a huge bite out of her toast to stop herself blurting exactly how much.

Coral tapped the article. 'You could do worse than marrying into that family.'

Gemma choked. 'Gotta go,' she mumbled, snatching up the keys in one hand, juggling her bag and toast in the other.

Thankfully, her mum merely waved as she backed out of the door.

She wasn't the marrying kind. She'd have to let a guy get close enough for a relationship first, and that was as likely as her taking up spear-fishing.

Even if she took the risk, getting hitched to a millionaire bachelor who didn't do romantic entanglements would be the last thing she'd do. High-maintenance, rich designer guys weren't her type.

If she kept telling herself long enough, she might start to believe it.

Rory sat through three early-morning meetings, drank four cups of espresso and ate half a bagel, clock-watching the entire time.

Not that heading to the Portsea site for an impromptu visit would lessen his uneasiness. If anything, seeing Gemma would exacerbate it.

He'd been horrified when he'd blurted the invitation to work all day Saturday, second-guessing himself in a way he never did in the business arena.

He shouldn't have kissed her.

Since when did he give in to impulse? Never.

He'd succumbed twice now: first when picking her up, then on that picnic.

Another huge *faux pas,* organising the picnic. He'd seen her nerves the night before, when she'd bolted after her presentation, and thought it might put her at ease to be out in the open rather than pacing her room waiting for the investors' decision. With the added bonus of confronting his baffling attraction for her and getting it out of his system.

His motives had been pure. His execution? Lousy.

He should have known a picnic would throw them together in an intimacy that made him squirm. She'd asked him why he'd kissed her when he'd picked her up. He'd responded by kissing her again, properly this time. Schmuck.

Throw in that awkward, revealing little chat about their parents and he mentally kicked himself—hard.

He could blame his lunacy on any number of factors: his admiration for her work ethic and chutzpah, his attraction to her intelligence and understated beauty, his genuine excitement following her presentation about what she could bring to his project.

In reality, he'd blurted the truth when she'd asked: she intrigued him, like no woman had before.

That was what had prompted his invitation for them to spend Saturday together, work or otherwise. He'd done it out of desperation, cloaked in business terms, because he feared he didn't want to go a whole three days without seeing her.

Not good.

Then he'd spied the newspaper in his periodicals pile and guilt had ripped through him when he'd seen evidence of his plan coming to fruition.

His father and the associated negative press for Devlin Corp had been wiped from the gossip columns, replaced by news of his appointing Gemma, as he'd intended, with

the added bonus of their other luxury developments mentioned. The kind of positive publicity money couldn't buy.

Seeing the half-page picture of her taken from her CV,
reading the accompanying article, he should have been
stoked.

He'd achieved what he'd wanted: establishing her as
the face of his new development, showing the country
Devlin Corp cared about the environment, and hopefully
guaranteeing he wouldn't run into the same problems his
dad had up at Port Douglas.

Instead, all he could do was stare at that picture and
the way Gemma glowed. Even in a grainy professional
shot, eyes wide and bordering on startled, her hair loose
and mussed, she captivated him.

Which meant he'd have to do his damnedest to keep
things strictly business. Getting involved with Gemma
would be messy, and he didn't have time in his life for
mess—not when Devlin Corp was finally starting to kick
corporate ass.

He'd never mixed business with pleasure, had deliberately avoided dating anyone in his work sphere because of
the possible complications and fallout. And there *would*
be fallout. That was a given.

The women he dated always said they weren't interested in anything heavy at the start, but once they'd pro-
gressed past the first few dates the claws were unsheathed,
ready to hook into him and not let go.

While Gemma didn't seem the type, with her transient
job and London base, he didn't want to botch this opportunity. He had a top-notch marine expert willing to ensure
his Portsea project dotted all the *i*'s and crossed all the
t's. The mansions would be environmentally certified as
well as lavish, guaranteeing top dollar for those wealthy
few lucky enough to afford them.

He'd be a fool to jeopardise all that for the sake of a self-indulgent fling.

As his marketing manager droned on about a new campaign he studied the newspaper article again, via the search engine on his smartphone.

He didn't want to use Gemma, but the phone had rung off the hook this morning—land-owners from Cairns to Launceston, enquiring about Devlin Corp's luxury development packages, asking for quotes. It was the first time in six months they'd had this kind of buzz, thanks to Devlin Corp showing its eco-friendly side.

People were environmentally conscious these days: forgoing plastic shopping bags, composting, recycling, using water tanks, harnessing solar energy. They didn't take kindly to large corporations felling trees and churning land, as his dad had found out on the rainforest fringe in Port Douglas.

Seeing a marine environmental scientist associated with his beachside project would bring kudos to his company and boost profit margins, without drawing unwanted attention from protestors.

Win-win.

Then why the nagging guilt that he'd unwittingly drawn her into this and she'd be furious if she knew?

He shut down the article and hesitated, his thumb poised over the keypad. He needed to keep Devlin Corp front and centre with positive publicity, needed to ensure the public saw Gemma doing what he'd hired her for.

Blowing out a long breath, he brought up his in-box, firing off an e-mail to his PA. Denise knew the drill. She'd leaked his whereabouts to the press at opportune moments over the last six months, claiming to be 'an unnamed source' when the company needed a boost or was desperate to counteract Bert's bad publicity.

Time for his 'source' to let the press know where Gemma would be on Saturday.

Gemma's morning had been manic: inspecting the beach, revising plans, going over new energy sources, scoping out the beach surrounds to ensure the managers knew where the amendments were to take place.

The guys had been nothing but professional, and she'd been buoyed by their acceptance of her. Until the boss man roared up in his Merc mid-afternoon and they scattered, leaving her to face him alone.

Her throat constricted as he stepped from the car in a grey suit offset by a pale blue shirt and navy striped tie, his long strides closing the distance between them at a rapid pace.

For one crazy, irrational second she wanted to run to meet him. The thought alone was enough to eradicate her sudden breathlessness and have her focussing on work.

'How's it going?'

'Fine.'

He raised a brow at her abrupt response and she glanced away, pretending to study the markers already scattering the ground.

'Productive morning?'

'Uh-huh.'

An awkward silence descended and she shuffled documents, flipped through plans, studying them as if they held the answers to eternal youth.

'Still happy to work tomorrow?'

He'd lowered his voice, and its deep timbre strummed her like a caress, her body responding on a visceral level that scared the heck out of her.

'Yeah.'

If he was tiring of her monosyllabic answers he didn't show it.

'Great. I'll pick you up at your place around six.'

And have early riser Coral accidentally-on-purpose orchestrate a meeting? Not likely.

'I can drive.'

He glared at her VW. 'I don't think so.'

'I'll borrow Mum's car—'

'I'll be there at six.'

To her astonishment, he walked away, leaving her wanting to tell him what he could do with his orders.

But as she watched him meet up with a few of the managers and gesture towards the land, his animation obvious even at a distance, some of her animosity at his command waned. It made sense for him to drive. Car-pooling preserved the ozone. It wasn't *his* fault she couldn't stop thinking about him or those distracting kisses.

Judging by his authoritative behaviour, he hadn't given them a second thought.

Good. At least one of them was thinking clearly.

As for the potential problem with matchmaking Coral? Time to shout her mum a treat.

CHAPTER NINE

GEMMA didn't feel the slightest twinge of guilt when she bundled her mum off to a swanky South Yarra day-spa for a Saturday-morning facial.

Coral had been sweetly surprised and very eager to head out. After scribbling a nondescript note saying she'd be out all day and late back, Gemma flung a few essentials into her backpack and waited impatiently for Rory to arrive.

The faster they hit the road, the less likely she'd be to call today off. She'd been tempted—boy, had she been tempted. Seeing him yesterday on the job site after the picnic episode had erected an unseen wall between them; she'd been stilted and nervous, he'd been aloof and distant. Who knew how they'd manage to interact one-on-one today?

When his Merc slid to a smooth stop in front of the house she hitched her backpack higher and bounded down the path, eager to get underway.

She almost stumbled when he got out, walked around the car and opened the passenger door. His impeccable manners were not surprising, but the simple action reminded her of her dad. He'd always used to open doors for Coral and her—a small thing she'd forgotten until now.

Sadness lodged in her throat but she cleared it, pasting on a bright smile as she neared the car.

'Right on time.'

He gave a funny little half-bow. 'Was there ever any doubt?'

'Punctuality is part of the workaholic's handbook, so I guess not.'

The corners of his mouth twitched. 'Hey, I'm heading out of town for the day. Does that sound like a workaholic to you?'

'Considering you're heading out of town for *work,* that'd be a resounding yeah.' She pointed at the car boot. 'Bet you've got a laptop stored in there.'

'Care to sweeten that bet?'

'Sure.'

He hooked his fingers beneath the straps of her back-pack to help her shrug out of it, effectively trapping her, and she tried not to breathe in his addictive masculine scent.

'What did you have in mind?'

She pondered, while her imagination took flight, en-visaging him giving a little tug on the straps, bringing their bodies so close she could feel his radiant heat.

There were so many bets that sprang to mind, most of them X-rated, but she couldn't make a flirty joke—not when he hadn't cracked a smile yet. Regardless of that picnic kiss, they had to focus on business.

Tell that to her inner mischief-maker, hell-bent on get-ting Mr Conservative to lighten up.

'Okay, here's the deal. If there's a laptop in there, we get to play hooky for a while today. If there's no laptop, you work to your heart's content the whole day.'

At last a breakthrough. Interest flared in his eyes.

'Sounds doable. As long as you don't have me diving with sharks if I lose.'

'Would I do that?'

He shot her a dubious glance as he slid the straps off her shoulders and held the backpack in one hand as if it weighed nothing.

'Guess we better pop this boot and see who wins?'

'You're on.'

Gemma crossed her fingers behind her back. While she was all for work, they needed to lose the residual awkwardness from that kiss. If he was anything like her he'd retreated because of it, and the way they'd connected.

She hadn't expected his candour. Most guys would have lied about why they'd kissed her when she'd asked, even though that first kiss when he'd picked her up hadn't been particularly passionate.

But he'd revealed he liked her and his inherent honesty had blown her away. If she'd back-pedalled, too scared to lower her defences, how must *he* be feeling? A guy who confessed he didn't do complications would be petrified.

She'd withdrawn yesterday. He seemed determined to continue their emotional avoidance today. She couldn't blame him for it—not when she agreed—but the thought of spending her Saturday working with this tension between them didn't sound fun.

'Do you want to do the honours or should I?'

He held out the car's remote control. 'Go ahead. I wouldn't dream of depriving you of your fun and games.'

Annoyed by his impassivity, she grabbed the remote and hit the button, inadvertently holding her breath as the boot popped. When he raised it to place her backpack inside, she scanned the huge space: golf clubs, gym bag, no laptop.

Dammit.

He gestured towards the boot, the hint of a grin playing about his mouth. 'Well?'

Not giving up that easily, she pointed to the gym bag. 'Could be in there.'

'Why don't you open it and see?'

'And rifle through your undies? No, thanks.'

The imp in her rejoiced as he blushed and held up his hands.

'You win. My laptop's stored under the passenger seat.'

'Gotcha!'

She did a little victory shimmy, and at last he smiled.

'Fine. We get to play hooky *after* we've put in a solid six hours work.'

'Good. Even workaholics need to play every now and then,' she said, her gaze drawn to his mouth, remembering exactly how fantastic he could be while playing.

She'd never been a weak-kneed, belly-flopping female, but when she tore her gaze from his mouth, only to see the blatant yearning in his eyes, her knees shook and her stomach tumbled.

He'd given a resounding answer to her unspoken question as to whether he still felt the spark.

'You're playing with fire,' he said, his expression reverting to guarded as he closed the boot and guided her to the passenger seat, his hand in the small of her back gently supportive.

For a confirmed independent gal, it felt nice to be supported for once.

As long as she didn't get used to it.

'We're almost there.'

Gemma struggled to consciousness, trapped halfway between a luscious dream of waking up next to Rory and the startling reality of having his voice next to her.

'You've slept the whole way.'

Opening her eyes, she blinked, yawned and stretched, her confusion clearing as she remembered where she was.

'We're in Portsea already?'

'Yeah, easy drive without peak-hour traffic.'

'Did I really sleep the whole way?'

'The moment we hit the freeway about five minutes from your place.'

She grimaced and used her pinkie to wipe the gritty sleep from the corners of her eyes, before making a subtle dab around her mouth, hoping she hadn't drooled.

'Some travel companion I make.'

'The snoring was rather soothing after a while.'

Mortified, she couldn't look at him. 'I don't snore.'

'Keep telling yourself that.'

He chuckled and, glancing over his shoulder, turned left, slowing the car as he pulled into the project's make-shift car park. 'Next time I'm investing in a decent pair of earplugs.'

She whacked him and he laughed, the sound giving her hope that he'd loosen up after all.

In a way, falling asleep had been a bonus, as she'd avoided the small-talk nightmare they'd had on the way back from the Yarra Valley. Yet a small part of her couldn't help but wonder what would have happened if she'd been awake.

Would they have delved deeper into that *moment* they'd had outside the car at her place? Would they have moved beyond discussing their families onto something more meaningful, like their hopes and dreams? Or would he have retreated again? She'd bet the latter.

Stepping from the car, she stretched, marvelling at the view. The lights of the Mornington Peninsula twinkled in the early-morning dimness, curving around the bay like the fine diamonds on Coral's bracelet.

Thinking of her mum and the jewellery she could have sold rather than her dad's land if she needed money soured her mood, and she wrapped her arms around her middle.

'Cold?'

'A little,' she said, but her inner frostiness was from the loss of something emotionally valuable rather than the chilly sea breeze.

'You'll warm up soon enough.' She shot him a glance and he rolled his eyes. 'From work. What do you think? I'm going to jump you?'

She could always live in hope.

He compressed his lips, regretting his comment, but there was no disguising his eyes, darkened with desire, and her body flushed, warmth oozing through her like heated honey.

She knew what she wanted.

For him to slide his hand into hers and tug her towards him. For him to say *Screw work. Let's play.* For him to admit they'd started something neither of them might understand or want but couldn't deny.

She wanted to live in the moment, forget her inherent fears and insecurities and open herself to this guy in every way.

What she wanted was irrelevant, considering he didn't say a word as he spun on his heel and marched towards the site office, unlocking the door and entering without looking back.

So that was how it was going to be.

Well, he could retreat all he liked and bury himself in work—but later today, during their down time, she'd get him to unwind if it killed her.

CHAPTER TEN

RORY liked working weekends. Liked the peace and quiet while people bustled between sporting games and shopping malls and barbecues. Liked the amount of work he caught up on. Liked the ability to focus without interruption.

Sadly, that wasn't happening today.

Not entirely fair, as Gemma wasn't interrupting so much as distracting. His fault, not hers.

He glanced at her strolling along the beach and speaking into a Dictaphone, her head constantly moving as she looked around. She'd been a dervish of activity since they'd arrived at Portsea at seven-thirty, surveying the beach, making amendments to her recommendations, jotting notes.

He liked the fact she kept out of his way. Gave him time to figure out what the hell he'd been thinking, inviting her for the day to work.

Work? Right. What a joke.

Their word games, their sparring, their parry and retreat rammed home what he'd suspected. Today was about being with her rather than any great desire to work.

And keeping his hands off her was slowly but surely killing him.

He'd tried to be the epitome of the polite business acquaintance/friend, had tried to maintain a distance. But she'd undermined him with her silly bets and loaded looks and crazy earrings.

Those earrings really bugged him. Rose quartz sea lions today, their frivolity in stark contrast to the rest of her practicality. A woman who wore khaki cargoes, a brown T-shirt, beige hiking jacket and steel-capped boots shouldn't wear giddy earrings. They got him wondering... Would she be light-hearted and playful in other areas of her life, particularly the bedroom, once stripped of her practical armour?

Damn, he couldn't keep thinking like this.

He never second-guessed any decision he made. When he wanted something in the business arena he made it happen. No room for uncertainty. So why this burning desire to yell *Screw work,* sweep Gemma off her feet and head straight for the privacy of the sand dunes?

As if sensing his stare, she looked up and waved, her ponytail whipping in the gusty wind, her face glowing. Her clothes might be plain but in that moment, silhouetted against the morning sun, which gilded her hair and created a halo around her, she was the most beautiful woman he'd ever seen.

He returned her wave, knowing he should head back to the site office and type up some last minute ideas he'd had to improve driveway access. Instead he found himself heading down the rickety wooden steps to the beach.

She met him halfway and his chest almost caved with the weight of pretending they were nothing more than work colleagues.

His earlier assessment hadn't done her justice. Up close, he saw a faint pink flushed her cheeks, accentuating the incredible blue of her eyes, and her smile was a poleaxing combination of joy and wickedness.

'Was wondering when you'd give up on the boring stuff up there and head down to the beach where it's all happening.'

He couldn't help but return her smile. 'That "boring stuff up there" is what you're being paid to ensure doesn't impact on down here.'

She snapped her fingers. 'I knew I was here for a reason.'

He stared at the ocean, unable to bear her radiant smile a second longer. They needed to get back on solid ground, work ground, and forget the teasing—no matter how light-hearted. It would be his undoing.

He cleared his throat. 'What did you think of the amended plan on the high-end homes?'

Her right eyebrow twitched, the only sign she was surprised by his abrupt switch from playful to business.

'Love it.' Her gaze swung to the land on their left. 'Angling the upper storey will capture the sun perfectly, enhancing utilisation of solar power.'

'That's the idea.'

He followed her line of vision, imagining the finished product: opulent three-storey mansions, rendered pale mocha to blend in with the sandy surrounds, expansive floor-to-ceiling glass windows, contemporary angles adding uniqueness.

He loved the luxury homes Devlin Corp built, had admired them since he was a kid, when his grandfather used to take him from site to site. Back then he'd thought they were palaces fit for kings and queens. His parents' open plan home had been the signature design back then.

Pity the queen hadn't stuck around and the king had kept trying to fill her shoes with ugly stepsisters.

He was mixing his metaphors. Better than mixing business with pleasure.

'And dropping the water tanks underground is a stroke of genius.'

He couldn't help but be buzzed by her praise. 'They're a bit of an eyesore. Better not to detract from all this.'

He gestured towards the beach around them, and this time her eyebrow arched all the way.

'Careful, you're almost sounding human.'

'Just because I'm a businessman it doesn't mean I've lost sight of the bigger picture.'

He held up a finger when she opened her mouth to respond.

'But the sea wall on the highest point of the beach stays.'

She paled. 'But that will exclude the sand behind the wall from the normal onshore and offshore movement characteristic of normal beach behaviour.'

Making a wisecrack about beach behaviour at this point wouldn't be a smart move—not when her playfulness had vanished, replaced by five feet six inches of fervent, riled environmentalist.

'It could make the beach unusable for long periods after heavy wave action, and considering the people who'll live here that's sad.'

'There's plenty more beach access around here. It's only a small section.'

She sighed, her exasperation audible. 'You're already developing a park on the upper part of the beach. That's cutting off a vital reserve of sand for the beach during erosion phases, when the sand is moved off the beach by waves. Any sea wall, no matter how small, can lead to severe depletion of dune sand and ultimately no beach.'

While she'd kept her tone surprisingly calm, her chest heaved with the effort of her conviction. He wanted to bundle her into his arms and squeeze her tight.

He was proud of her—proud of her convictions, her knowledge, her dedication to preserving nature.

'Let me look over the proposed plans again and I'll see what I can do.'

Her answering grin had enough power to slug him where he feared it most: his heart.

'You get it, don't you?'

He held up a finger in warning. 'I said I'd take another look at the plans. If it's economically feasible, I'm willing to implement changes. You've already twisted my arm to include your marine conservation centre. Don't push your luck.'

She screwed up her nose. 'Yuck, you're going all corporate bottom-dollar on me.'

'I have investors to consider, shareholders too—'

'I know what'll convince you.'

She did a funny little dance that kicked up sand and he couldn't help but laugh.

'What are you up to?'

'Leave everything to me. This afternoon when we're playing hooky I'm taking you to meet some friends, and if they can't convince you to help preserve this beautiful marine environment, nothing will.'

'These friends aren't going to ply me with suspect cookies and homebrew before pushing me off a pier?'

'Wait and see.'

He didn't trust her exaggerated wink any more than his resolution to keep things between them casual.

Gemma slipped her mask and snorkel on, trying not to ogle Rory in his wetsuit. How the man managed to make rubber look good was beyond her.

He seemed unfazed by the whole adventure, and she wondered if anything ever rattled him.

When she'd procured bathing suits and they'd boarded the boat at Sorrento, he'd merely raised an eyebrow and settled in for the ride.

How many times had her dad brought her out here? Twenty? Thirty? She never tired of snorkelling at Popes Eye Marine National Park, a small semi-circle of rocks between Queenscliff and Sorrento. The shallow protected waters teemed with colourful fish and marine life, and today she'd get to share that with Rory.

Before the main event.

'Ready?'

He nodded and gave a thumbs-up. 'As I'll ever be.'

'You've done this before, right?'

He dangled his snorkel and mask on the end of his finger, swinging along with the gentle swell buffeting the boat. 'Snorkelling? Yeah. Here in the icy waters of Port Phillip Bay? Not on your life.'

'Trust me, it's worth it.'

Especially the way he was looking at her at that moment, with admiration and something deeper darkening his eyes.

They joined the group entering the water, and for the next half-hour stayed close as they snorkelled around the national park.

As a kid, she'd loved the fact this place had been constructed as an incomplete island fort during the late 1800s, and had imagined herself as a pirate, a sea captain and a mermaid—in that order.

When they finally broke the surface of the water Gemma pointed upwards, delighting in Rory's open-mouthed awe.

'There's a unique rookery of Australasian gannets around here. Watch this.'

A large gannet with an impressive two-metre wingspan

swooped fast, plunging into the bay at high speed. Rory held his breath, and she revelled in his surprise when the bird reappeared with a fish in its beak.

'They're excellent plunge divers.'

'I can see that.'

They bobbed in the water for a few moments, but this time he wasn't looking at the local wildlife. He had the strangest expression as he stared at her, as if he was seeing her for the first time.

The group leader gave a shout to round them up, and when she climbed back aboard she put the shivery feeling shimmying through her body down to the frigid water rather than the intensity of his stare.

'What's next?'

'You'll see.'

He didn't push her for info, content to sit next to her, close enough that their rubber-clad thighs brushed. Those shivers were tiptoeing down her spine with increasing frequency, making her want to snuggle into him.

A short time later he shifted and sat upright. 'Are those seals?'

'Uh-huh. Welcome to Chinaman's Hat seal platform.'

His genuine grin gladdened her heart. 'Are these your friends?'

'No, you'll meet them shortly. But you'll like these guys too—you have something in common.'

'We do?'

'Yeah. They're a bachelor community of Australian Fur Seals and they can get grumpy if approached.'

He laughed out loud. 'By "something in common", I'm hoping you mean we're bachelors?'

'And the rest,' she said, her sickly sweet smile garnering her a hip-to-shoulder bump.

'I'm not grumpy.'

She wondered how far she should take this, before deciding to give him another nudge. 'Maybe not grumpy. A tad withdrawn?'

His eyes clouded and she immediately regretted bringing it up out here and spoiling their outing.

'End of a long working week. I'm usually mellow.'

Mellow? Was that what he called a well-executed retreat?

'Uh-huh,' she mumbled in vague agreement.

She was a fool. What had she expected? For him to admit he was back-pedalling because he didn't want this to get complicated between them? For him to confess he was as scared as her of any emotional involvement but was sorely tempted regardless?

An awkward silence stretched between them and she plucked at the rubber stretched taut on her thigh. Then he said, 'Gemma, I don't want—'

'Dolphins!'

Once the cry went up everyone crowded to the side of the boat and the moment vanished.

As they re-entered the water, she wondered if he'd been about to say *I don't want complications, I don't want a relationship* or, the worst possibility, *I don't want you.*

Before she slipped on her mask and snorkel she waved at the small pod of Bottlenose dolphins nearby.

'Meet my friends. If they don't convince you to look after the local beaches, nothing will.'

Wisely, he remained silent, but the understanding flash in his eyes before he slid his mask on gave her hope.

They slipped into the water in small groups, and while they held on to mermaid lines and allowed the curious dolphins to come to them Gemma watched Rory.

She saw the first moment a dolphin swam within touching distance and his eyes crinkled at the corners in delight, saw the awe on his face when a group of five dolphins leapt out of the water, saw the workaholic executive melt away beneath the onslaught of these beautiful creatures.

When they'd finally made it back on the boat and stripped out of their gear it took him a full ten minutes before he spoke.

'I get it,' he said, his voice low, his tone reverent, and she refrained from flinging her arms around his neck and hugging the life out of him—just.

She settled for touching his hand. 'I'm glad.'

He turned his hand over, sliding his fingers between hers, holding on tight, and that was how they remained for the return journey to Sorrento.

Holding hands, her head resting on his shoulder, watching the sun set in a dazzling display of mauve and gold and pink, streaking the sky with beauty.

Gemma didn't believe in romance or fairytales or happily-ever-afters. But this? It came pretty darn close to topping her list of life's perfect moments.

CHAPTER ELEVEN

Rory had swum in the crystal clear ocean around the Maldives, had snorkelled in Fiji and dived in the Caribbean with Bert on a rare child-friendly trip in his early teens. But nothing beat the swim he'd had today.

Initially unimpressed by the icy waters of Port Phillip Bay, he'd quickly warmed up—courtesy of Gemma's wide-eyed enthusiasm and her 'friends'.

The laughs had been on him when he'd realised his vision of dreadlocked hippies was in reality a pod of dolphins.

Devlin Corp donated to various conservation causes, but he'd be lying if he didn't admit that had more to do with tax breaks than any real love of marine wildlife.

Gemma had opened his eyes today, and while he wouldn't be diving into that shiver-inducing water on a regular basis, he knew he'd take a more personal role in his company's causes.

What he'd seen on that dolphin dive—her enthusiasm, her animation, her verve—had reaffirmed that marine science wasn't just a job to her. She truly believed in the cause and her ethics blew him away.

He couldn't fathom how he could have been attracted to women who were torn between the Caesar salad and the wonton soup, women who valued their six-hundred-dollar pairs of designer shoes more than the ozone, women who prided themselves on etiquette and appearances but were shallower than the rock pools where the boat had docked.

Being with Gemma, her refreshing honesty and exuberance and lack of pretence, made him feel like a new man—a man capable of handling a spontaneous, vivacious woman, a man capable of change.

He couldn't remember the last time he'd played hooky. He was rarely sick and never lolled around. The closest he came to relaxing was the occasional sauna at the gym, and even that had him edgy after fifteen minutes.

Spending the afternoon swimming with dolphins should have had him going stir-crazy. Instead he'd loved it. Gemma had intrigued him from the start, and now, after discovering another side to this incredibly multi-faceted woman, he knew he was in serious trouble.

He'd bounded up the wooden steps of the Baths Café in Sorrento, where they were stopping for a snack before heading home, when his phone buzzed.

He'd left it in the car all afternoon: another first. He never went anywhere without his phone—needed to be connected to his business at all times. Yet he hadn't given Devlin Corp a second thought all day and that sobered him.

He was acting just like his dad. Putting personal needs first, acting on a whim, forgetting the implications for Devlin Corp.

Hell.

He'd sworn never to be like Bert—had made a commitment to Devlin Corp. So what was he doing, losing his head over a woman who would be out of his life sooner rather than later?

Annoyed at his afternoon lapse, he scrolled through

the messages. He tensed when he spied the latest from his PA Denise.

Check out the Melbourne Daily late edition.

With a few taps on his bookmarks he brought up the online paper and flipped through the pages. On page eight, in full Technicolor glory, was a picture of Gemma talking into her Dictaphone on the beach this morning: focussed, wind-blown, magnificent.

He skimmed the article, vindicated by the numerous mentions of Devlin Corp and its continual rise to the top, interspersed with the story of the company's dedication to the environment in hiring Gemma. They extolled her virtues at length, listing her credentials and how her presence at Portsea Point would ensure marine viability alongside Devlin Corp's signature homes.

He'd got what he wanted. Bert and his associated bad publicity for Devlin Corp had been wiped from the media, replaced by Gemma as the face of his new project. Positive spin all the way.

As his gaze focussed on that picture of Gemma in her natural glory, doing what she loved best, he wondered at what cost.

With Devlin Corp at stake he'd done what he had to do. But how would Gemma feel about it? Technically he wasn't using her, merely boosting her profile as the company's latest and greatest consultant, but would his genuine motivation count for anything when he told her the truth?

With her waiting for him inside the café, guilt twanged his conscience—hard. He should tell her. It was the decent thing to do.

Turning off his phone for the first time ever, he stuck it in his pocket, mentally rehearsing what he'd say, how he'd explain his rationale without sounding like a jerk.

By the time he pushed through the glass door and caught sight of her, sitting on the veranda, all his good intentions flew out of the open window.

Her hair fluttered in the breeze like gold silk, and her eyes were wide and sparkling, reflecting the stunning blue of the bay behind her, as she caught sight of him and waved.

His resolve shot, revelations forgotten, he strode across the café, focussed on nothing but being with her.

Gemma never lazed around. She spent every moment of every day at high velocity, packing as much into her life as she could. She liked being busy at work, liked the satisfaction of a job well done. In her down-time she hiked and swam, preferring to keep moving.

The guys she'd dated hadn't been interested in her frenetic pace. They'd preferred women to sloth around, lazing by a pool in a bikini rather than actually swimming. Guys who needed attention, guys so blatantly wrong for her she often wondered if that was the reason she'd dated them.

She'd never had the grand dream of settling down and getting married and raising a family, was too used to hiding behind the job she loved to avoid the pain of emotional involvement. Too used to her independent lifestyle, too used to packing up at a moment's notice and traversing the world for work. She thrived on it and, while many might call her selfish, she liked her life just fine.

Getting to know Rory had changed all that.

It made no sense.

She hadn't known him long.

He was a corporate big-wig; she was an environmental specialist.

He liked designer duds; she liked cheap, functional and funky.

They were light years apart in every way.

Yet seeing him come alive in the bay this afternoon, watching him open his eyes and his heart, see her for who she really was and what mattered, had shattered her illusions for ever.

It was okay to have the happily-ever-after dream with the right person.

Unexpectedly—catastrophically—she'd found him.

The guy she could see herself changing her life for.

A guy special enough that she could stay in Melbourne and build a life with him.

A guy worthy of investing in emotionally for the first time.

It wasn't one specific thing but the whole package: his ability to make her laugh, to say the right thing, to make her feel like a beautiful woman with a glance.

She didn't need compliments to feel good about herself; growing up a tomboy and working in a male-dominated environment, she was used to being one of the boys.

Facials, manicures and hair straighteners were as foreign to her as sequins and clutch bags and stilettos. Yet spending time with Rory made her feel more feminine, more appreciated, than she'd ever been.

The question was, what was she going to do about it?

She had a job to do on the Portsea project; that much was clear. Once the month was up? What then? Rory expected her to pack up and leave, a job well done. Should she tell him she might stick around?

The implications of a revelation that momentous made her shiver.

'You cold?'

Rory sat beside her and draped an arm across her shoulders, rubbing her arm to warm her up. Holding hands on the boat after sharing the dolphin swim had changed something between them, breaking down his barriers, bringing them closer in a way she'd never expected.

He'd been more relaxed than she'd ever seen him, unconsciously touching her in unspoken agreement that he liked her despite not admitting it.

They were a fine pair: dancing around each other, emotionally stunted, terrified to take the first step. After that ride she felt as if they'd taken a leap into a scary abyss.

'Not any more,' she said, snuggling into him as if it was the most natural thing in the world, giving him a clear signal that she'd like to do this on an ongoing basis.

'Fancy another coffee?'

'No, thanks. I'm content to sit awhile if you are?'

'I'm exactly where I want to be,' he said, his expression inscrutable as he stared out at the choppy bay, at small waves created by a blustery wind.

Over two lattes each, and a massive blueberry muffin for her, all-day breakfast for him, they'd watched the ferry from Queenscliff dock and depart again, people strolling along the beach, kids playing in the icy shallows.

Gemma could have sat there all evening, letting the world pass her by, but as Rory's arm remained wrapped around her she knew she had to tell him.

Someone like him didn't come along every day and she'd be a fool to pretend otherwise. They might not have a lot in common, and she knew next to nothing about him, but she'd taken risks her entire life. What was one more?

The fact previous risks had been physical and this risk was emotional? She'd waste time second-guessing that later.

'Rory?'

'Hmm?'

Reluctant to move, but needing to see his reaction when she dropped her bombshell, she eased back and he removed his arm. She missed the contact, and emboldened by her decision, she placed a hand on his thigh.

'I'm thinking of sticking around.'

Confusion creased his brow for a second, before realisation widened his eyes.

'In Melbourne, you mean?'

'Uh-huh.'

His thigh flexed beneath her palm, and she resisted the urge to stroke the firm sinews.

'Once this job is finished, I might look around for something else to work on. What do you think?'

For a horrifying second panic flared in his eyes, before his lips curved into a smile.

'I think that's a great idea.' He covered her hand with his.

She waited for him to say more, waited for him to say it would give them a chance to get to know one another, waited for him to say he was willing to take a chance if she was.

His silence unnerved her, but he hadn't released her hand so she'd have to be happy with that. What had she expected? For a self-professed commitment-phobe to jump for joy?

It had taken *her* long enough to get to this point. She needed to give him time to get used to the idea that they might share more than a spark.

'Good.'

She had the impression he wanted to say something, but a waitress came to clear the table and the moment passed.

'We better make a move.'

A chill settled over her as they stood. It had little to do

with the wind and more to do with the nagging feeling that, despite his words, her declaration had scared him more than he let on.

Coral usually spent Saturday evenings having dinner with friends. Gemma was counting on it as Rory dropped her off, but one glance at the driveway had her giving him a hurried kiss.

Coral's Honda sat in front of her VW, meaning at any moment her mum would come waltzing out on the pretext of checking that a possum wasn't devouring her roses, or some such guff, when in reality she'd want to scope out Rory. Gemma could only imagine how inadequate Coral might make her feel about spending time with someone as smooth and suited as him.

'Today was great. We got heaps of work done, and you were a trooper on the dolphin swim, and the café was lovely, and—'

'Is anything wrong?'

Darting a quick glance over her shoulder, and seeing an upstairs curtain twitch, she grimaced. 'My mum's queen bee on the local gossip grapevine. She thrives on it. So I'm trying to beat a hasty exit and leave you unmolested before she descends.'

He laughed. 'She can't be that bad.'

'Worse.'

Harsh, and not entirely true, but the last thing she needed right now was her mother crossing paths with Rory and the inevitable comparison and judgement that would follow.

'Will I see you Monday?'

The moment the question fell from her lips she inwardly winced. Since when had she sounded like a needy female?

'Actually, I'll be tied up in meetings Monday to Wednesday, then I'm heading interstate towards the end of the week.'

'Right.'

But it wasn't. Things were far from right. Since she'd declared her plans to stick around he'd been acting strange. Nothing overtly obvious, but a subtle withdrawing that left her wondering if she'd misread the afternoon and feeling more than a little hurt.

'I'll call you when I get back.'

'Sure.'

She snagged her backpack from the backseat and leaped from the car before he could say anything else. She'd heard enough for now.

When he didn't try to kiss her again, or touch her or speak, she held her head high, hitched her backpack higher, and strode towards the house.

Not having a clue about relationships sucked. Emotionally clueless, she had a sinking suspicion she'd made a mess of the best day of her life.

Rory tooted as she reached the front door and she waved, glancing over her shoulder in time to see him pull away. Could he leave any faster?

Tension banded her forehead with the promise of an incoming headache, and she patted her pocket for her key—only to have the door swing open.

On the bright side, Rory had left.

On the down side, Coral hovered on the other side of the door like an avenging angel, clad in head-to-toe Chanel and waving her in like a signaller waving in a jet on an aircraft carrier.

'You've got some explaining to do, my girl.'

Gemma rolled her eyes and trudged inside. 'At twenty-nine, I don't need to justify myself to anyone.'

Coral placed a hand on her shoulder. 'I'm teasing.'

Great. Now parting with Rory had her edgy. She heard the uncharacteristic tremor in Coral's voice and, hating taking her mood out on her mum, she dumped her backpack on the floor.

'I'd kill for a peppermint tea.'

Coral's genuine smile made her feel like a cow. 'Coming right up.'

Gemma followed her mum into the kitchen, determined to give her the bare basics, scull her tea, and head for her room where she'd grouch and grumble and mull in peace.

'How was your day?'

'Good.'

'You were with Rory?'

'Uh-huh.'

Maybe if she kept up the brief responses Coral would move on to another topic.

Fat chance.

'Portsea must've been chilly with that southerly today.'

Gemma's head snapped up. 'How did you know I was in Portsea?'

'Honey, everyone knows.'

Her expression benign, Coral pushed the late edition newspaper across the counter and she snatched it, flicking through the pages with flustered fingers.

There she was again: page eight, on the beach early that morning. She looked a mess, ponytail whipping in the wind, Dictaphone shoved to her mouth, her eyes squinting against sand and sun. She'd never looked good in photos and this one proved it.

'Did you read the article?'

She rolled her eyes and did just that. Most of the article centred on her expertise and what she brought to the project, along with singing Devlin Corp's praises.

The thing reeked of a PR stunt—as if someone at the company had fed some gossip-hungry journo her where-abouts, a few choice lines, and they'd run with it.

'Does it bother you, being in the media?'

Tossing the paper away, Gemma shook her head. 'Not really.'

Coral poured boiling water into teacups and dangled the bags. 'Was it just you and Rory at Portsea today?'

'Mum, drop it.'

Sliding a cup across the bench, Coral perched on a bar stool opposite. 'You're awfully touchy.'

That tended to happen when you finally took the plunge and put yourself out there, and the guy you thought was into you didn't return the enthusiasm.

Knowing she'd have to give her mum something, she shrugged. 'We worked most of the day, then chilled out. Nothing serious.'

Coral raised a knowing eyebrow. 'You never had a boyfriend growing up. You've never mentioned anyone on your brief visits home. Now you seem to be spending a lot of time with this guy—'

'Stop.'

Gemma slid off her stool so quickly she almost up-ended the scalding tea. The sensible thing to do would be to zip her lips and march out of there, take time to cool off. But the uncertainty and second-guessing of the last few hours coalesced into an anger directed at the person in front of her—a person who had no right to start acting maternal now, after years of making her feel worthless.

How she'd yearned for these questions as a teenager, when she'd never fitted in at school but wanted to, when she'd needed her mum's advice on boys and make-up and clothes but didn't know how to ask, when she'd craved her mum's approval and support.

The lack of support had hurt. It was a hurt she'd locked away and kept hidden beneath an outer layer of bravado and boldness. A hurt that had festered. And having Rory pull away from her, just as her mum had pulled away all those years ago, brought back her insecurities in a rush: maybe she wasn't girly enough, wasn't beautiful enough, plain wasn't enough?

Shaky and out of her depth, she jabbed a finger in Coral's direction. 'Tell me this. Why the interest now? You never gave a damn when I needed you most.'

She spat each word out, punctuated with the underlying hurt she'd buried deep now bubbling to the surface.

'You pushed me away, Mum. Rejected me. And I had no idea why.'

Coral staggered as if wounded, adding to Gemma's guilt, but the pain of neglect and wishing things had been different flooded out in a torrent she couldn't control.

'It's a bit late to pull the caring act now. Where were you when Dad died, when I really needed you? And all those years after, when I needed some kind of acknowledgement you loved me? Where was the concern then, huh?'

Coral plopped down onto the bar stool, her face a deathly white.

'I—I—don't know what to say…'

'That's just it. When I needed you most, you never did.'

Clutching her churning belly to stop herself being sick, Gemma turned and ran.

CHAPTER TWELVE

RORY had botched Saturday.

Big-time.

He hadn't told Gemma the truth about those newspaper photos. And he sure as hell hadn't told her the truth about how he was feeling.

Therein lay the problem, because damned if he knew.

As much as he liked her, as much as he wanted to explore what they'd started with their spasmodic flirting, he'd freaked out when she'd said she was sticking around.

Not that she'd spelled out exactly why, but he knew. By the softness around her mouth when she told him, by the unguarded zeal in her eyes, by the hope on her face, he knew she was doing it for him.

He couldn't handle that much responsibility.

Shove him into the CEO's chair at an ailing company? Yep, he could cope with his eyes closed. But being responsible for someone's feelings? Hell, no.

He'd grown up independent, taking care of himself from an early age, learning not to depend on anyone. It suited him.

Deep down, he knew this freak-out was probably based on some long-buried rebellion against his parents—a mother more wrapped up in her art than him for the first five years of his life before she bolted, and a father who paid more attention to his constant parade of unsuitable girlfriends.

He'd accepted his dysfunctional family as a kid with resignation, but he'd be kidding himself if he thought his upbringing hadn't left a lasting legacy.

He wanted to be nothing like his parents.

Didn't want to let a woman close for fear of letting her down like Bert did. Didn't want to get emotionally involved for fear of finding it too claustrophobic and bolting like his mum.

The only problem was his deep-seated fear of emotional attachment might cost him a woman he could seriously fall for given half a chance.

He'd been so blown away by her declaration he'd backpedalled, desperate to buy time, deliberately staying away an entire week.

Sadly, time away hadn't changed the situation. He needed to acknowledge the truth. They'd connected on some innate level that defied logic or explanation, and he needed to recognise it or lose her.

Considering he'd mucked up appointments, turned up late to an interstate flight and made a general cock-up of things over the last week, he couldn't lose her.

He'd missed her that much.

If losing her wasn't an option, he had to face facts. Was he ready for a real relationship? What were his expectations? What were hers?

If she stuck around, for how long? Would she flit off at the first opportunity if a great job offer came her way? If so, how would that affect them?

Too many questions, not enough answers; none beyond his wild speculations.

They had to talk.

After he finished grovelling.

* * *

This had better be good.

Gemma pushed through the glass door and entered the vegetarian café, wondering what surprised her more: the fact Rory had called or his choice of meeting place.

Until she realised he probably assumed because she was an environmentalist she was vegetarian too. Considering she'd barely managed to nibble on a cheese scone at their picnic, followed by a blueberry muffin at the Baths Café while he devoured fried eggs and bacon, she could understand how he'd make the leap. She'd save her carnivore side for another time; *if* there was another time.

True to his word, he'd been busy all week. Too busy to call or e-mail or text. No one was *that* busy.

She'd pretended not to care. She'd worked harder and longer than everyone else, stoked by her plans for energy efficiency and marine conservation and reducing carbon footprints at Portsea coming together.

During the day and well into the evening she didn't have time to dwell on Rory's rationale. But at night, when she lay on her back and stared at the ceiling, she'd rehashed every second of Saturday afternoon, wondering how she could have misread the situation.

The tiny bell over the door tinkled and the skin on her nape prickled. She knew who'd entered behind her without having to turn around. Crazy how in tune they could be after knowing each other a fortnight.

'Thanks for coming,' he said, placing a hand in the small of her back. The barest pressure sent an instant zap of awareness through her.

Her brain might know there was no future for them; try telling that to her body.

'No worries,' she answered, aiming for blithe, sounding ridiculously perky instead.

He guided her through the small tables, choosing the

corner booth furthest from the door, ensuring privacy. That figured. He'd start off with, *It's not you, it's me.*

He picked up the grease-stained menu, gave it scant attention before sticking it back between the salt and pepper shakers.

'You hungry?'

'Not really.'

'Me either.'

He clasped his hands together, rested them on the table. Combined with his sombre expression, he looked like a judge about to give an unfavourable ruling.

Considering the surprising ache in her chest, she was probably not far off the mark.

'I had this spiel worked out—'

'Let me save you the hassle. It's okay. I get you're not into me, that you're not interested in complications. Don't worry—'

'I'm into you.'

She only just caught his muttered *'Way too much to be good for me.'*

For the first time all week her mouth curved upwards.

'You could sound a little more enthusiastic.'

He frowned. 'Sorry, I'm making a hash of this again.'

She could make it easier for him, but after the week he'd put her through? Not likely.

He leaned back in his chair and hooked his clasped hands behind his head—a powerful businessman out of place in this tiny café in a Melbourne side street. What really commanded her attention was the play of emotions across his face: uncertainty, regret, hope. She focussed on the hope.

He took a deep breath, blew it out through pursed lips. She waited.

'You threw me.'

He wasn't the only one. She'd done a fair job of shocking herself the last fortnight.

'You come across as this independent, fearless, in-control woman who travels the world and muscles her way into jobs and doesn't like permanency. And that suited me just fine.'

He ruffled the top of his hair, spiking it. 'I liked you, but after the way we'd been flirting, then how we connected on the boat, hearing you say you were sticking around...' He shrugged. 'I kinda freaked out.'

'I noticed.'

Some of the tension drained from his rigid shoulders when she didn't snap, and he lowered his hands, stretching his neck from side to side like a boxer about to enter the ring.

'I guess what concerns me is you're giving up some of your freedom.'

He didn't add *for me* but he knew. Knew how much her independence meant—knew what she'd be sacrificing if she stuck around. For him.

'I don't play games. That's why I gave it to you straight. I like you. I want to spend some time exploring the spark we share. I'm not *giving up my freedom* for anyone. This is for *me*.' She clapped a hand to her chest. 'It's what *I* want to do.'

Admiration glittered in his eyes but she wasn't finished.

'I can't give you any promises about how long I'll stick around, and I'm certainly not angling for a commitment, but for the next few months I want to stay in Melbourne.' She pointed at him. 'To hang out with you.'

He snagged her hand and brought it to his lips, pressing a kiss in her palm and curling her fingers over it. She needed little encouragement to hold on to a kiss like that.

'There's something else—'

'Do I really need to hear it? Because right now we're in a good place.' She waved her free hand between them. 'If you're going to disturb that, leave it.'

He hesitated, the frown between his brows only finally easing when she pulled a face, imitating him.

'Don't look so serious. We're dating, not getting married.'

She couldn't blame him for chuckling in relief.

'Am I allowed to say *anything?*'

'Only if it's good news.'

His smile faded. 'The building commencement date has been moved forward. They start Monday.'

While she'd known this day was coming—heck, she'd been working towards it with a team—it didn't make the reality any easier. Her dad's land was being carved up. And there wasn't one damn thing she could do about it.

'In a fairytale world I'd give you back the land if I could. But there are too many people's livelihoods invested in this project—people's jobs, millions of dollars—'

'You don't have to justify this. You bought the land fair and square, and I gave up believing in fairytales a long time ago.'

She tried to sound matter-of-fact, but her voice quivered and he clasped her hands across the table.

'You mentioned you used to camp out there with your dad. How about we do that this weekend?'

As a distraction technique from her misery, it worked.

'Seriously?'

He nodded. 'Give you a chance to say goodbye.'

A chance of closure, to farewell her favourite spot in the world, to move on in her mind. She'd never forget how safe Portsea made her feel, its familiarity warming her as much as her memories, but her haven would soon be gone and she needed to come to terms with that. It made sense. But did she really want to share a guaranteed poignant, sad and potentially blubbery weekend with Rory?

Sensing her reticence, he squeezed her hands. 'Or, if you'd prefer, you camp out there alone. Though it's mighty lonely along that stretch of beach and I'd probably worry—'

'Fine. You can come.'

She rolled her eyes—an effective move against the sting of tears.

'Though I have to warn you there's this wombat that used to attack us, and he had a few feral wallaby mates. Then there's the snakes and redback spiders and—'

To her amazement, he paled.

'You've been camping before, right?'

Being a typical male, he squared his shoulders and uttered famous last words. 'How hard can it be?'

CHAPTER THIRTEEN

'NEED some help?"

Rory straightened and clutched at his middle back. 'No, thanks, I'm almost done.'

'Right.'

Gemma sent a pointed glance at the storm clouds gathering, before staring at his lame attempt at pegging the tent.

He frowned and turned his back on her, hefting the mallet high over his head and bringing it down with a resounding thud. It skidded off the peg and landed on his boot.

He cursed, and she turned away in case he looked up and caught her smiling. It wasn't her fault the guy had to go all macho on her—especially when he'd never been camping before.

In a way it was very sweet, him giving her the opportunity to camp here one last time. It had touched her in a way she hadn't expected—especially coming from a business-oriented guy who wouldn't have a sappy bone in his body. But he really should have let her take care of everything instead of divvying up tasks.

She understood he needed to feel in control. Typical guy. But judging by the time it had taken him to struggle to this point in erecting the tent, perhaps he should've assigned that particular task to her. Goodness only knew what he'd packed in the way of food.

'Isn't there something you should be doing?'

'Nope.'

She dusted off her hands, earning a filthy look. 'I've scooped out a fire pit, set up the kindling and a metal grille over it, and strung up some rope for tarps in case we need it.'

He frowned and glanced up into the trees. 'Why would we need tarps? That's what the tent's for.'

Not wanting to dent his manly pride, already suffering under the hatchet job he was making of the tent, she shrugged.

'The weather forecast sounded grim, so thought it'd pay to be doubly prepared.'

He grunted in response and resumed his mallet-swinging.

Funnily enough, she hadn't been camping in ages, and sharing this experience with him meant a lot—despite her constant teasing.

She knew he'd offered because he felt bad about the building date being brought forward, but it had been inevitable anyway. Whether the bulldozers arrived on Monday or next month made little difference. Her sanctuary would be irreversibly changed for ever.

Her light-heartedness in teasing Rory faded. Thinking of her refuge being demolished brought Coral to the forefront of her mind—a place she didn't want her to be. She'd avoided her the last week—had stayed out late working at the office and waited until she'd heard her mum head for her morning walk to shower and slip out.

Childish, but their last confrontation had been ugly, and freshly fragile after having Rory MIA for a week, with no contact, she hadn't been up to it. She regretted her harsh words, wished she hadn't verbalised the pain lodged in her heart all these years.

What would change in discovering why her mum had rejected her all those years ago? It wouldn't bring back those lost years, when she would have given anything for a hug or a genuine smile or maternal support.

She liked the fact they'd been getting along better this trip, that her mum had been making an effort. It reminded her of the good times when her dad had been alive, when Coral would roll her eyes at their woodworking and experiments yet ply them with lemonade and cookies while she made frequent trips to the shed to chat or offer inane advice they'd all laugh at.

Or the times her mum would sit in the stands at the local pool while her dad coached her in butterfly and freestyle and backstroke, encouraging her to be faster than the boys' swim team.

Or the times they'd indulged her passion for hiking, when her mum would wait patiently in the car for hours while she raced her dad up the highest peak.

While shopping and gossiping at cafés held little interest for her, Gemma would have done it if her mum had invited her along.

Sadly, verbalising her rejection hadn't helped and she regretted blurting the truth and the devastation on her mum's face when she'd stormed out.

She wanted to make amends but didn't know how. If they hadn't been able to breach the gap after her dad died, how would they recover from this?

But the small part of her that still craved her mum's attention, the part she'd deliberately shut down years ago, couldn't be ignored and demanded she make peace.

If she planned on staying in Melbourne she'd have to make an effort to repair the damage, to get their relationship back on civil terms. But she had to get out of the house—couldn't risk another potential blow-out tearing them apart completely.

She'd investigated a few short-term rentals yesterday, and expected to hear back on Monday. Until then her date was erecting the Taj Mahal of tents.

Glancing over her shoulder, she checked his progress and stifled a laugh. The tent resembled a lean-to rather than a monument.

She could offer to help, but considering his prickliness earlier he'd take it as a slight on his manly pride and refuse.

Her time would be better spent doing really important stuff. Like putting the finishing touches on her surprise. She reached for her mobile to do just that.

Rory prided himself on his construction skills. He might spend his days behind a desk, but he had a set of tools bestowed upon him by his grandfather that the old guy had taught him to use. He knew his way around hammer and wrench and screwdriver, had replaced worn washers and fixed busted water pipes, and he'd constructed a rudimentary workbench at home.

But this tent business? Major pain in the ass.

He'd read the instructions online after purchasing it. Looked simple enough. But he'd soon learned getting the damn walls to stay upright while he hammered in pegs was tougher than it looked. What he'd anticipated as being a fifteen-minute job max had taken him an hour, and the thing still looked lopsided.

As long as it kept them sheltered it would do its job. He'd wasted enough time when he could have been with Gemma.

He flicked a glance in her direction and his chest contracted. She sat in the passenger seat of his car, her feet curled beneath her to one side, engrossed in her phone, one thumb tapping a text message, the other hand absent-mindedly twirling the end of her ponytail round and round a finger.

No make-up, clad in jeans and a loose sweatshirt and hiking books, she looked like the sexiest woman he'd ever seen.

He'd been a fool to almost lose her because he couldn't handle feeling like this.

He could use all the excuses in the world—his parents' disaster of a marriage, his grandfather throwing out titbits of affection sparingly, his never having been involved in a long-term relationship—but they were just that: excuses.

He had the power to control his destiny, so why this inability to let Gemma into his heart? No one to blame but himself. He knew why too.

Plain, old-fashioned fear. Fear of losing control, fear of not being in command, fear she'd get to know the real him and run a mile.

That was the clincher: he might have an ounce of Bert in him and drive her away, as Bert had driven away his mother all those years ago.

Not that he was a philanderer, like his dad, but he'd seen beneath Bert's suave veneer over the years and the fact was Bert couldn't commit. To anyone or anything. He had power and prestige and looks, could command a room with a tilt of his head, but there was an inner cool-ness women found irresistible and yet it prevented him from growing close.

Rory felt the same way. Apart from Devlin Corp, he'd never felt truly passionate about anything.

Until now.

That was what really scared him—that once he'd al-lowed himself to truly feel for the first time, and if the relationship went pear-shaped and Gemma left, he'd be sapped of some of his strength and the power that made him invincible in the business arena.

Stupid? Maybe. But for now he'd shelve his fears and make the best of it. In it for a good time, not a long time, and all that jazz.

As if she sensed him watching her she glanced up and smiled. That slow, sexy curving of her lips called him to action.

He flung down the mallet and strode across the distance between them, squatting next to the open door and snagging her hand. 'What're you doing?'

'You'll see.'

He entwined his fingers with hers, noting her short nails, ragged cuticles, the lack of polish, finding them more appealing than the many manicured talons he'd artfully dodged over the years. 'A surprise, huh?'

'Something like that.'

Her eyes twinkled with mischief and he'd never wanted to kiss her more. 'When do I get to see this great surprise?'

She glanced at her watch and screwed up her nose, pretending to think. 'In about an hour, when it's dark.'

'Sounds intriguing.'

She squeezed his hand. 'If you finish that tent super-quick, might be in forty-five minutes.'

'Slave driver,' he said, his mock grumpy tone eliciting a laugh.

'And don't you forget it.'

His gaze swung to the pathetically lopsided tent and he cringed. He'd rather be with her, but if they planned on sleeping he'd better fix it.

Then again, perhaps there were other perks to not sleeping tonight?

* * *

'Ready?'

He nodded, his admiration for the amazing woman by his side tinged with unstoppable desire. How the hell he'd keep his hands off her tonight he had no idea.

'Should I be worried?'

She pretended to ponder, her eyes crinkling, her pert nose screwed up, and he'd never wanted to kiss anyone as much as he wanted to kiss her at that moment.

'Depends. If you're scared of the monster from the deep coming up the beach to gobble you at night, then maybe you *should* be afraid.' She wiggled her eyebrows. 'Very afraid.'

Snagging her hand in his, he tugged her down the final steps to the beach. 'I'm willing to risk it if you are.'

'Hey, I'm not the one who'd never ventured into Port Phillip Bay before.' She bumped him with her hip in an intimate gesture he liked. 'Deep-sea monsters are particularly attracted to newbies, and seeing as it was your first time in the bay last week…'

All he could focus on was one word: *attracted*. He was intensely, irrationally, imploringly attracted to her.

His self-proclamation to keep this weekend about her saying a proper goodbye to the land she loved and keeping his libido in check was in serious danger—not helped by the fact she'd brought him to a deserted beach for a moonlit walk.

'They wouldn't dare come near me with you by my side.'

She stopped and placed a hand on a cocked hip. 'Are you saying I'm scary?'

'No.'

'Then what *are* you implying?'

He loved this playfulness and her inherent ability to make any situation fun.

'You're a sea nymph. No monster in his right mind would mess with you.'

Her lips curved into a devastating smile and he knew right then he was in trouble—big trouble.

Not the kind that could be dismissed, but the kind he'd have to confront if he wanted to sleep again some time this century.

'Come on, your surprise is ready.'

Curious as to what she had in store, he fell into step alongside her, slowing down his strides to match hers, content to stroll.

He never strolled. He power-walked or jogged or strode, always moving at a chaotic pace. *You snooze, you lose* had been his motto for so long he'd forgotten what it was like to slow down and take a good, long, hard look around.

Who knew you could snorkel in Port Phillip Bay? Or that seals and dolphins and a plethora of wildlife were out there, waiting to be appreciated?

As for the Portsea land Devlin Corp had snapped up for a bargain price—he never would have fully appreciated it if Gemma hadn't come on board. He was proud of the luxury mansions his company constructed, proud of every single development around the country. But having her insight, her expertise, had opened his eyes to environmental issues he'd previously overlooked despite hiring specialists.

Portsea was only a two-hour drive from Melbourne, and yet the only time he'd ever visited was for the annual summer polo day. As for walking on this beach? Try never.

He liked his life, liked the frenetic pace and cut-throat energy of the corporate world, but this camping weekend with Gemma was teaching him something. It was okay to chill. Not that he'd become hooked on it or anything, but maybe he'd be making more trips to the beach in the future.

They rounded a small headland and he gaped.

'Surprise.'

She bounced on the balls of her feet, the white of her teeth reflected in the campfire on the beach.

'How did you manage this?'

'Called in a favour from one of dad's old fishing buddies.' She tugged him towards the fire, where her contact had left a cooler, and glanced at a rocky crop overhead and waved. 'Chester's a crabby old bachelor but he has a weakness for soap operas, so when I asked him to prep a fire on the beach for me he threw in this as well.'

'This' happened to be a cooler stocked with expensive champagne, strawberries and chocolate.

'A closet romantic?'

'Like you?'

'My fridge has three ingredients. What do you think?'

She laughed. 'Let me guess. Mouldy cheese, long-life milk and a six-pack of boutique beer—the classic bachelor staples.'

'Don't knock it till you've tried it.'

He picked up the bottle and made quick work of the cork, surprisingly piqued by a twinge of loneliness. He rarely cooked, hence his barely stocked fridge. When he ate he had an ordered-in snatched sandwich at his desk or a business dinner where he didn't taste the food while wrangling problems.

Being a bachelor suited him, but Gemma made it sound as appealing as soggy seaweed on toast.

'I've tried it,' she said, holding out the plastic flutes she'd dug up from the cooler. 'I lead a busy life, rarely in one place for long, so I guess your fridge has three more items in it than mine usually does.'

He poured champagne into the flutes and stashed the bottle on ice when he was done, not wanting to get into the deep and meaningful with her but curious about her life.

'Do you ever wish for stability and a picket fence and kids?'

She thrust a flute at him and retreated a step. He guessed he had his answer.

'Why? Because I'm a woman?'

'No, because you've got a lot to give. The way you throw yourself into work. The way you care about the environment and marine life. You'd bring that same passion to a family.'

He'd rendered her speechless.

He blundered on. 'Don't mind me. The stress of constructing that tent is making me ramble.'

She sank to the sand and patted a spot next to her—a spot he was all too willing to take. Better than having her kick sand in his face for raving like a lunatic about private matters no concern of his.

'When things matter to me I give them my all.' She twirled the flute, and tiny shards of flame reflected off the champagne. 'Always thought I'd never have time for a family.'

She downed half her champagne, lowering the flute to pin him with a probing stare.

'Why the questions? Bachelorhood not living up to expectations? Secretly pining for a family?'

'Hell, no.'

'Would you like some time to think about that?'

He managed a rueful chuckle, wondering why he felt so empty inside. Devlin Corp was his life. Anything else would be a complication he didn't need.

He'd seen first-hand what having a distracted father

meant to a family: a neglected wife who eventually left, and a kid who learned far too young to fend for himself.

He'd never make the same mistakes his dad had. So why did his instant vehement refusal leave him hollow?

'I'm not a family man,' he said, and the champagne left sourness in his mouth as he wondered what madness had possessed him to head down this track.

'You're nothing like your dad,' she said softly, her touch on his hand scaring him as much as her insight.

'I sometimes wonder.'

Her fingertips flittered across the back of his knuckles, and he shuddered with the effort not to ease her back onto the sand and cover her body with his.

'Wonder what?'

Unaware where his urge to unburden his soul was coming from, he clamped his lips.

She didn't pressure him for answers. Her fingertips continued their leisurely exploration, unhurried.

One of her many qualities he liked was the absence of the usual female necessity to badger, to know everything. She wouldn't have asked unless she genuinely cared for his answer, and that more than anything loosened his lips.

'I wonder if I'm like Bert after all.'

Her fingers stilled, rested over his, the warmth from her palm reassuring.

'Not professionally, because I know we're nothing alike there, but in our personal lives.'

'You haven't been married four times.'

'No, but at least Bert connected with those women long enough to want to marry them.'

'Couldn't have been much of connection—' She stumbled and he raised an eyebrow. 'Except with your mum, I mean. He must've loved her. They had you.'

He smiled at her blunder. 'It's okay. I'm just musing

out loud. Forget it.' He turned his hand over and threaded his fingers through hers. 'Now, how about we dunk those strawberries?'

'Later.'

She scooted closer until she pressed into his side and they sat in silence, staring into the fire.

Her closeness, both physically and emotionally, should have scared him, but he found himself relaxing, drunk on her warmth and openness rather than any alcohol buzz.

'Guess we all have our self-doubts,' she said, drawing spirals in the sand. 'You don't want to be like your dad, and I wish I was more like my mum—but that's impossible.'

He laid his hand over hers. 'You mentioned at the picnic you thought she rejected you because you weren't worthy?'

Her lips thinned and a tiny crease appeared between her brows. 'All in the past.'

He picked up her hand, turned it over and traced the lines in her palm, wanting to distract her, wanting to eradicate the sorrow in her voice.

'You shouldn't do that.'

'What?'

'Doubt yourself—ever. You're amazing, Gemma. I admire everything about you, from your work ethic to your spontaneity—' he gestured at the fire '—and everything in between. You're more than worthy. You're incredible. Don't let anyone make you think otherwise, okay?'

She mumbled an agreement, the quaver in her tone ensuring he gave her time to gather her emotions. When the silence stretched to uncomfortable, it was time for a topic change, and he squeezed her hand.

'Thanks for taking me on that dolphin swim last week. I can't stop thinking about it. It was a real eye-opener.'

She cleared her throat. 'You're welcome.' She tilted her face up to him, her skin glowing in the firelight. 'Your adaptability surprised me.'

'You didn't think I'd like it?'

'Let's just say I have a newfound respect for a guy who can swap a designer suit for a wetsuit and still manage to look exceptionally cool.'

'You think I'm cool?'

'Hot, more like it.'

She held his gaze, her eyes sparking with daring. Daring him to cross the line, daring him to kiss her, daring him to go for it.

The fire crackled. Waves crashed. He resisted.

This was it. The definitive moment where he crossed a line in the sand—literally.

If he kissed her now he wouldn't stop. Not this time.

'I warned you once about playing with fire,' he said, his free hand reaching up of its own volition to cup her cheek.

Defiant to the end, she half turned her head, nipping the pad of his thumb and sending heat streaking to his groin.

'I can handle it if you can.'

With one gigantic jump, he leapt over his metaphorical line and didn't look back.

Gemma lived in the moment.

She'd always been a daredevil, but losing her dad had cemented her reckless streak. Life was too short to waste. It was a mantra she lived by daily. A mantra that had her knees wobbling ever so slightly as she strolled across the sand hand in hand with Rory.

She had a million thoughts whirring through her head,

ranging from *I hope that tent holds* to *With this kind of tension this promises to be the best sex ever.*

Despite being opposites, they'd connected on so many levels, and tonight, by the fire on the beach, he'd revealed more than she could have hoped for.

Rory Devlin really understood her. He'd honed in on her feelings of rejection in the past and said exactly the right thing. She *was* worthy. Worthy of a guy like him. And the fact he liked her for who she was, without artifice, without pretence, had ultimately lowered her emotional defences.

She wanted to be close to him. In every possible way.

After their revealing chat he'd tortured her, holding her hand, cupping her cheek, staring into her eyes...and not kissing her.

She'd willed him to close the distance between them, to ravage her lips as he'd done previously on that memorable picnic. Instead he'd leaned so close their breaths had mingled, increasing anticipation, before moving his mouth towards her ear. Where he'd proceeded to tell her in great detail what they'd be doing tonight.

All night long.

They'd doused the fire so fast she hadn't had time to grab a torch and, laughing, they'd grabbed the cooler and made a run for their camping area.

Her body buzzed, her knees shook, her senses were on high alert. To his credit, he didn't break stride as they all but ran across the sand, and when she stumbled he caught her.

'Nice save.'

His fingertips grazed the sliver of skin exposed between her jeans and T-shirt where it had ridden up.

'Can't have you breaking a leg now. Not with what I've got planned for tonight.'

The bold declaration hung in the air between them, brash, provocative. Barely restrained tension was zapping between them, creating more energy than any solar panel.

Her skin prickled with it—a sensuous tingling that made her want to strip off and bare her body to the faint moonlight.

'Show me.'

Without saying another word Rory slid an arm around her waist and backed her through the unzipped tent flap towards the airbed, his slow, leisurely perusal like an intimate caress.

As moonlight spilled into the tent and the breeze cooled her skin Rory peeled her clothes off, worshipped her body and made love to her until she almost passed out from the pleasure.

Living in the moment had a lot to be said for it.

CHAPTER FOURTEEN

GEMMA had been a conscientious camper in the past. She'd ensure the tent had been erected properly, she'd check the food had been sealed properly, and she'd anticipate possible problems before they happened.

But she'd never camped with a sexy distraction before—and therein lay her downfall.

After making love twice they'd gleefully tumbled into their sleeping bags, spending a blissful few hours in each other's arms, only to be awoken at dawn soaked to the skin.

'You did fasten the fly?'

Rory sent a quick glance in the direction of his groin and she rolled her eyes.

'The fly for the tent. The sheet that goes over the tent to stop condensation on the inside and to keep it rainproof. In case of bad weather.'

His shamefaced expression said it all. 'Told you I'd never camped before.'

'Yeah, but...'

No use blaming him. She should have checked it. And would have if he hadn't started kissing her and the rest...

Wriggling out of a squelching sleeping bag and the wet tent, she tried to think quickly.

'I could erect the tarp, but we're already soaked.

Hopefully it was a passing shower and we can dry off before—'

'Freaking hell!'

Her jaw dropped as Rory started hopping around as if a bee had bitten his butt.

'What's wrong?'

He pointed towards his feet and downgraded his hopping to hobbling.

'Something's attacked the soles of my feet.'

She winced in sympathy. 'You fell asleep with your bare feet outside the tent?'

He nodded and muttered another curse. 'The tent's too small for me, so when you dozed off I stuck my feet out the end of the tent.'

'You've probably been bitten by bull-ants.' She gestured towards a wet log. 'Take a seat. Let me see.'

Glaring at her as if this was all her fault, he sat and presented his soles for inspection. And promptly lost his balance and fell backwards into a hole. A grumbling hole.

'What the—?'

He struggled to get upright—only to come face to face with a growling wombat the size of a baby elephant.

Okay, so she was exaggerating, but the way Rory had paled she should amend her analogy to stegosaurus size.

'What do I do?' he breathed, scrambling backwards on his hands and sore soles, doing a fair crab imitation.

'Don't worry. Willemena won't hurt you.'

'Won't hurt me? She's growling at me like I'm supper.'

'You disturbed her snoozy hidey-hole. She has every right to be upset.'

Rory tried to keep on eye on the wombat while giving her a death glare. 'You're siding with this creature?'

'"This creature" has lived here for years. The workers have probably been feeding her or leaving food scraps.

That's why she's hanging around here. She's made a shallow burrow near our campsite because she's expecting food.'

His eyebrows rose further the longer her explanation lasted, and she stifled a laugh.

'You fell on her while she was snoozing. I'd be growling too if I got woken like that.'

He eyeballed the wombat, which took a waddling step towards him.

'She can't hurt me, right?'

'Those claws have been known to rip a man apart, but you should be all right.'

With another mumbled curse he managed to gain purchase on his sore soles and surge to his feet—only to start hopping around again.

Willemena—or more likely her offspring, though Gemma had left out that part—lost interest when no food was forthcoming and trundled off in the direction of the bush.

Smiling, Gemma swung her gaze back to Rory, and in that instant, with his wet jeans clinging to his legs and his hair mussed, his mouth compressed in an unimpressed line, her heart flipped over without a hope of righting itself.

She loved him.

Loved this man for all his intriguing facets: the powerful businessman, the commanding lover, the flexible guy who had accepted her chained to his precious display, camped on her dad's land for the first time, the guy who truly understood her and liked her for it.

Their gazes met and his mouth relaxed, curving into a rueful smile that confirmed it.

How could she *not* love a guy who tolerated getting drenched, getting bitten and getting an up-close-and-personal encounter with a wombat, and still managed to smile about it?

She flew across the space between them and flung herself into his arms, wrapping her arms around his waist and burying her face in his chest.

'If this is a sympathy hug, maybe I should get tortured by the local fauna more often.'

She didn't answer, hugged him tighter, and her heart sighed with the rightness of it when he held her close as if he'd never let go.

She could always wish.

When Gemma steered his Merc into the underground car park of his penthouse and killed the engine he sent a silent prayer of thanks heavenward.

Aborting their camping trip should have made him guilty, but with his feet still stinging, despite a liberal dosing of calamine lotion, and his ego still smarting from making a fool of himself, all he felt was relief.

A nice hot soak in his Jacuzzi followed by a night tucked up in one-thousand-thread-count sheets with Gemma by his side sounded a lot more appealing than roughing it.

'Home sweet home,' she said, handing him the keys. 'How are the feet?'

He wiggled his toes. 'I'll live.'

She grinned. 'Remind me never to take you to the Amazon. The pythons, the killer tarantulas—'

'I get the picture.' He snapped his fingers. 'If we're heading in that direction, how about we skip the Amazon and head for Rio instead? *Carnivale?* Great beaches? Top hotels?'

'You're such a wuss,' she said, shaking her head, her soft smile making something twist in his chest.

But I'm all yours, he wanted to say, needing to tell her how much she meant to him but unsure of the words.

He was kidding himself if he thought they weren't in this for more than a fling. Which meant before they went any further he had to tell her the truth. He took a deep breath.

'I need to tell you something.'

'Let me guess. You're planning on standing on a scorpion nest next, or crawling up a tree to wake a rabid koala?'

There was no easy way to say this. He searched for the right words, came up empty, and settled for the blunt truth.

'I orchestrated that publicity about you in the newspaper.'

Her smile faded. The joy in her eyes was replaced with wariness and disappointment and disgust.

'Why?'

'For the company.'

'The company?' she parroted, her tone eerily flat.

It terrified him.

'My dad's constantly in the paper, flaunting some totally inappropriate woman, making a laughing stock of himself and the company—'

'And you decided to use me to oust him and take centre stage?'

He nodded, ashamed he hadn't told her sooner. 'Devlin Corp was headed for disaster when I took over from dad six months ago. We had problems with protestors on that other job and the media constantly dredges it up. I needed to raise our environmental profile and you came along at the right time.'

Her eyes narrowed, sparking blue fire. 'I get it. Hire

the eco-warrior, tout her association with the company constantly, get your money's worth. So *did* you?'

Her face had crumpled, and she made a god-awful strangled sound that slugged him.

'Gemma, listen—'

'What I want to know is was I an *inappropriate* woman too?'

She spoke over him, as if she hadn't heard a word he'd said, and by the impenetrable mask settling over her face he knew he was in trouble. Nothing he could say or do would get through to her.

'Is that what our relationship's based on? You start something with me so once the papers get tired of my professional qualifications they can plaster us over the stupid society pages?'

Her voice wobbled and he reached for her but she slapped his hands away, her shoulders rigid.

'Tell me this. Was this weekend just some dumb publicity stunt too? Get me onside as part of your ruse? Should I expect to see pictures of our beach campfire or worse spread across the papers tomorrow?'

'Course not.'

'I don't believe you,' she murmured, and turned away to stare out of the window, but not before he'd seen the shimmer of tears.

Those tears slugged him as much as her lack of faith in him. His grandfather hadn't believed in him—not really. Preferring to hand the company over to his flaky dad rather than the kid he'd groomed.

His dad hadn't believed in him either. He'd given him a year before Devlin Corp was bankrupt, but slapped him on the back regardless, with a jolly 'Don't worry, son. Business isn't everything.'

His dad was wrong. The family business *was* everything to him. It had been all he'd had. Until Gemma. Now she didn't believe in him either, and that hurt most of all.

His grandfather's lack of faith? Almost expected. His dad's? Foregone conclusion. Bert didn't have faith in much beyond Jack Daniels and the next warm bed.

But Gemma? He'd grown to value her opinion, grown to treasure those moments when she looked at him as if he was a giant among men.

He'd grown to love her.

The revelation slammed into him like a kick to the gut, leaving him just as winded.

Blindsided, he stared at the woman he loved, wanting to tell her all of it, desperate for her to understand his motivations, but unsure how to make her believe.

He needed her to believe in him.

'Gemma?'

She half turned towards him, a blond strand curling over her cheek, her top teeth worrying her bottom lip as she deliberately averted her eyes.

'I love you,' he blurted, cringing at his delivery but frantic to get the words out there, for her to hear him out.

Before he could say anything more she muttered, 'I don't believe that either,' flinging open the door and making a run for it.

CHAPTER FIFTEEN

FOR a girl who never cried, hooking up with Rory-bloody-Devlin had made a true mockery of her.

Gemma sobbed all the way home in the car, thankful she'd left her VW at his place.

Everything they'd shared had been a sham. He'd hired her for positive publicity and to deflect environmental lobbyists; he would have had to keep her sweet and what better way than to charm her and woo her?

Every tender moment they'd shared flashed before her eyes: his sweet, tentative greeting kiss when he'd picked her up for the Yarra Valley jaunt, the passionate picnic kiss, holding hands on the boat, making love in the tent.

Had it all been a lie? A calculated ploy to keep her on-side so his all-important damn company could complete the Portsea project on time?

Her anger rose exponentially as her sorrow petered out. By the time she'd battled Chapel Street traffic and pulled into her driveway she was ready to thump something.

Stomping into the house, she headed straight for the coffee machine. Not that she needed to be any more wired, but she was desperate to do something familiar to soothe her rampant fury.

And she *was* furious: furious at Rory for lying to her,

furious at him for using her, but most of all furious at herself for falling in love.

There were reasons she didn't take risks with her emotions, and this all-pervading, cloying, utterly soul-shattering devastation was one of them.

She enjoyed her life too much to feel this crappy, and from what she'd seen with colleagues over the years the moment you let love into your life was the moment you said goodbye to clarity and perspective and independence.

She should be thanking Rory for snapping her out of this so called love before she really invested her heart.

More than she already had.

She slammed the cupboard shut and plonked a cup on the counter, glaring at the coffee machine in the futile hope it would produce coffee sooner.

When it didn't, she whirled around to head for the fridge. And her gaze clashed with Coral's.

Great—that was all she needed. Another draining confrontation.

Unable to speak past the lump in her throat, she waited for her mum to speak. Instead, Coral stepped into the kitchen and opened her arms.

Gemma froze.

When was the last time her mum had embraced her? At the funeral? At the wake?

Too much had happened for her to want comfort from a mother who hadn't been available when she'd needed her most, but in that moment, looking into her mum's understanding eyes, she needed a hug more than she would have thought possible.

She took a few hesitant steps, stiff-legged and awkward like a colt, before Coral met her halfway, bundling her into her arms.

The sobs in the car were nothing to the tears tumbling down her cheeks now.

She had no idea how long her mum smoothed her back and murmured 'Shh…' in her ear, but eventually her tears ran out and she was left feeling awkward and embarrassed.

Coral didn't give her time to dwell. 'Sit. I'll make coffee.'

For once Gemma did as she was told, waiting for a barrage of questions that didn't come.

Finally, when she couldn't stand the silence any longer, she blurted, 'I've fallen in love with Rory Devlin.'

Coral didn't spill a drop of milk as she topped up the stainless steel jug.

'I figured as much.'

'How?'

Coral shrugged. 'The only time I've seen you cry is over your father, so I assumed this had to be over another man.'

Gemma didn't know if that made her sound like a weak female but she left it alone. Her mum was being nice, they'd glossed over their last confrontation, and she was dying for that coffee.

'What's the problem?' Coral placed a steaming cappuccino in front of her and took a seat opposite.

'He used me.'

Coral's eyes narrowed and her lips thinned. This evidence of her mum's protectiveness meant a lot.

'How?'

'He only hired me for my credentials, not my skills. Then he tipped off journos about me for good publicity in the paper for his precious bloody company, and got close to me to keep me onside.'

Coral nodded. 'Smart lad—trying to go one up on

Cuthbert's antics spread over the tabloids for all and sundry to see.'

Gemma gaped. 'You're *agreeing* with what he did?'

Coral's exasperated sigh blew the froth off her cappuccino. 'From a business perspective only.' She wiped the froth with her fingertip. 'From a personal viewpoint, I don't believe he used you for a minute. He cares about you. Any fool can see that.'

'How would you know?'

Shock number one had come when her mum had offered her a comforting hug. Shock number two blew her away now, as Coral slid open the third drawer of the dresser—the one that had used to house rubber bands and paperclips and recycled plastic bags—and pulled out a bulky scrapbook with her name on the cover.

'Here. See for yourself.'

Coral flipped towards the back of the scrapbook and pointed at a carefully clipped picture of her and Rory at the campsite yesterday, of him squatting next to the open car door, gazing up at her and holding her hand.

He'd lied.

She'd asked him if their camping weekend would be media fodder too. He'd said no.

She should have known better than to believe a word from his devious mouth. A guy who'd used her from the beginning would say anything to squirm his way out of trouble—all in the name of protecting his precious company.

'If that's not the expression of a smitten man, I don't know what is.'

Speechless, Gemma ignored the picture of Rory and flicked back through the scrapbook, her mind reeling as she scanned pages filled with her earliest drawings, the first Mother's Day card she'd made, a short story she'd written in second grade, yearly school photos, sporting achievements, the invitation to her graduation...

She'd known about the kiddie stuff, but all these clippings of her achievements after her dad had died? News to her.

When she came to the last page, the one with the newspaper clippings about her and the latest addition with her and Rory, she finally risked glancing at her mother. The woman who'd cared a lot more than she'd ever admitted.

'Why did you keep all this stuff?'

Coral tried to appear as poised and cool as ever, but Gemma noted her hands trembling as she picked up her coffee cup.

'No bull, Mum. The truth.'

Taking several long sips that grated on Gemma's nerves, Coral finally replaced the coffee cup on the table.

'Because I was proud of you, and it helped me feel close to you after your father died.'

The sip of coffee Gemma had taken soured in her mouth. Had her mum wanted to get close but hadn't known how?

'What do you mean, you couldn't get close to me?'

Coral paled and the corners of her mouth drooped. 'Maybe this isn't the best time to have this conversation—'

'There'll never be a good time.' Dragging in a breath, Gemma blew it out slowly, calming. 'You want me to start? Fine. After Dad died an invisible wall sprang up between us and I never knew why. Then I see this—' she waved at the scrapbook '—and it makes a mockery of every self-doubt I've ever had. So 'fess up. What's this all about?'

Anguish clouded Coral's eyes before her head sagged in defeat. 'Your father.'

Of all the answers Gemma had expected that hadn't been one of them. 'What does Dad have to do with this?'

Coral clasped her hands tightly and laid them in her lap, squaring her shoulders as if readying for battle. Her rigid posture was the epitome of prim and proper, without a hint of the defeat of a few moments ago.

'You were always your father's daughter from the time you could walk, and I could never compete with that.'

Shocked at the admission, Gemma shook her head. 'We were a close family. We did stuff together all the time. There was never a competition between you.'

'That's because I fitted in with whatever you wanted to do with your dad.' Coral's hands twisted, the knuckles stark white against her crimson suit. 'As a toddler you were already building block towers and pushing dump-trucks and demolishing trains. You weren't interested in dolls or fairies or sparkles. Then as you grew you trailed after your father constantly, spending hours locked away in that workshop of his. Shutting me out,' she added, speaking so softly Gemma almost didn't hear.

A pang of guilt shot through her misery. *Had* they shut her out? Gemma remembered rushing through her homework so she could spend a few hours after school watching her dad build something. And weekends had been heaven, when they'd lock themselves away in the workshop or trawl markets for parts.

Gemma had always thought her mum didn't mind because she'd watch them and ply them with snacks—when she wasn't busy hosting a garden party or having coffee with her friends on Chapel Street.

But maybe Coral had done those things to occupy her time? To fill the void left by a husband and only child so wrapped up in each other's hobbies they'd ignored her?

'We never meant to exclude you,' she said, the guilt

pressing more heavily against her chest when Coral blinked back tears.

'I know. And it didn't matter so much when we were a family. But after your father died...' Coral wrung her hands, twisting them over and over, until Gemma reached out and stopped her. 'I was afraid.'

'Of what?'

'Of having nothing in common with you, of not being able to relate to you in the same way you'd always related to your father, of having you reject me.'

Coral sniffed and dabbed her nose with a tissue while Gemma absorbed the enormity of the truth and regretted they hadn't had this conversation years ago.

'By the time I'd dealt with my grief and pulled myself together the gap between us had grown and I didn't know how to breach it.'

What could Gemma say? She knew exactly what her mum meant because she'd felt the same way. Wanting to be closer to her mother but not knowing how to approach her, especially when they had nothing in common. But if her mum could confess her innermost fears, so would she.

'I was only a teenager, Mum. I felt like I'd let you down in some way.'

Coral shook her head fiercely. '*Never.* I hate that you think you weren't good enough in some way. I never meant to reject you, darling. I was always proud of you.' She nodded at the scrapbook. 'That's proof of it...' Her mum trailed off, unable to meet her eyes.

'There's more, isn't there?'

Coral's teary gaze snapped to hers, her nod reluctant. 'I'm ashamed to admit I was jealous.'

'Of me?'

'No, of your relationship with your father. When you

hit your teens I expected you to grow apart from him, like my friends' kids, but you didn't. You two seemed to get closer, and that really irked.' Her gaze dropped to focus on her wringing hands. 'I—I thought it was me, that I was at fault somehow.'

'Mum—'

'No, let me finish.' Coral dabbed at her eyes, not a tell-tale blob of mascara to be seen. 'Losing your father ripped me apart, but in my own twisted way I thought it'd bring us closer. I didn't expect you to share my love of fashion or manicures or glossy magazines, but I wanted us to be close. When the opposite happened I didn't know how to deal with it.' Coral dragged her tear-filled gaze to meet hers. 'I let you down and I'm sorry.'

Gemma didn't know what to say. Not that she could say anything with that giant lump of regret stuck in her throat.

'You needed me after Karl died and I wasn't there for you. By the time I wanted to be it was too late…'

'It's never too late.' Gemma reached across the table and covered one of her mum's hands with hers. 'We can't change the past but we can make more of an effort in the future. We can both be there for each other.'

But, considering her relationship with Rory was over, would she still stick around?

'I've planned on staying longer in Melbourne once the Portsea project wraps up…'

Panic flared in Coral's eyes at the mention of Portsea, igniting Gemma's latent anger.

'I have to tell you, Mum, I'll never understand how you could've sold Dad's land for your own needs.'

Coral gnawed on her bottom lip, removing the carefully applied lipstick and leaving an ugly smudge.

Puzzled by her conflicted expression, Gemma removed

her hand, but Coral's hand snaked out and snagged hers, her eyes suddenly bright and clear.

'It wasn't for me.'

'What do you mean?'

'I sold the land to pay off your father's debts.'

Shock ripped through long-held belief. 'What about your lifestyle? This house?'

Coral squeezed her hand and released it. 'Your father's family bestowed this house, the Portsea land and some shares on us when we married. We lived off those investments. But your father insisted on sending you to private school, and he spent a lot on those experiments of his…'

She trailed off and the reality of the situation hit. Her mum hadn't sold Karl's land on a whim; she'd done it out of necessity.

'Are you in financial trouble now?'

Coral shook her head. 'The sale of the land cleared your school fees debt and paid off the rest of what we owed.'

Now stricken with guilt, Gemma said, 'Why didn't you tell me? After what I said to you, what I accused you of—'

'Because I didn't want to taint the image you had of your father. You idolised him, were devastated when he died. Better you should think I sold the land out of self-ishness than blame him.'

Her mum was *that* selfless? It only made what she'd thought that much meaner.

Anger mingled with regret. Anger at her dad for putting them in this predicament, anger that the perfect father she'd adored hadn't been so perfect, anger that her memories of him would now be tainted by disillusionment.

Anger at herself for blaming her mum for something that wasn't her fault.

'I'm sorry, Mum. For everything.'

Tears glistened in Coral's eyes again. 'I'm sorry too. For wasting all those years when I should've made more of an effort to reconnect with my only child.'

Gemma had never been a hugger, but embracing her mum now seemed the most natural thing in the world.

When they'd resumed their seats, Coral tapped the scrapbook.

'If you're in such a forgiving mood, maybe you should extend some towards that young man of yours?'

Gemma's reluctant gaze fell on the photo of Rory. He *did* have a starry-eyed expression, as if she was the best Christmas present he'd ever received. Probably an act, but damn, it was a good act—one she'd fallen for.

'I'm not only upset because he used me.' She knuckled her eyes, annoyed at the persistent burn of tears since she'd discovered the truth behind their relationship. 'It's more than that. I told him about *us*—how I felt worthless and not good enough when you rejected me.'

'Oh, honey, I'm so sorry—'

'It's okay, Mum, we've discussed it. We're moving on. But I opened up to Rory, the first guy I've ever trusted, and he's done the same thing. I thought he saw beneath my bravado, saw the real me and liked me for it regardless. But it was all a lie.'

A sob bubbled up and she swallowed it, determined not to cry over him any more.

'He doesn't respect me for who I really am. All he sees is what I can do for him professionally. He doesn't know me at all.'

That was what cleaved her heart: the fact he'd said she shouldn't doubt her self-worth, she was amazing, incredible, blah, blah, blah. And all the while he'd been buttering her up, getting cosy to suit his own ends.

He'd done exactly what she'd divulged had hurt her most: rejected her for no other reason than being herself.

She could throttle him.

'How did you find out?'

'The louse told me.' She breathed deeply, in and out, calming. 'We had this amazing weekend, connected on so many levels, then he blurted the truth.' Her hands fisted. 'I could kill him.'

'I'd help you if I thought he'd done what you're accusing him of.'

Gemma frowned at her mum's defence. 'He did it. He told me.'

'Why would he have told you the truth unless you mean something to him? He could've continued the lie but he didn't.'

Probably couldn't sleep at night with a guilty conscience. How she wished that wombat had gnawed on his bits.

'I'm not wasting time figuring out his motivations.'

Coral pursed her lips, deep in thought. 'Maybe you should? We've wasted a lot of years doubting ourselves, second-guessing, unable to reach out for fear of rejection.'

Coral touched her cheek in brief reassurance.

'Shouldn't you challenge him and hear his rationale, so you'll have no regrets whatever happens?'

Gemma sulked. Great time for her mum to pull out the maternal advice—especially when it made perfect sense.

'Take it from someone who knows. Don't waste a minute of your life wishing you could change a situation without giving it a damn good shake-up first.'

Was it that simple? Should she confront Rory? Give him a chance to explain?

She'd been so consumed by hurt when he'd told her the

truth she hadn't wanted to hear any more, let alone some misplaced declaration of love.

But what if he *did* love her? Could they make this work?

Only one way to find out.

Raising her coffee cup in Coral's direction, she smiled for the first time in an hour.

'Here's to more wise motherly advice.'

Coral's lower lip wobbled in response, a fat tear plopping into her coffee before she returned a watery smile.

Gemma couldn't cry any more. She'd used up her yearly quota. Tears were wasted.

Having her mum's reassurance meant the world to her: she *was* special and unique and loved—not some freakish outcast as she'd misguidedly thought all these years.

The knowledge gave her confidence. Confidence to confront her future head-on.

CHAPTER SIXTEEN

CONSIDERING he'd had his feet ravaged by killer insects, his ass almost chewed by a crazed wombat and his declaration of love flung back in his face over the weekend, Rory knew the week had to get better.

It didn't.

He spent Monday troubleshooting in Brisbane, Tuesday schmoozing in Sydney, and Wednesday delegating in Adelaide. Three full-on days of check-ins and airline food and Devlin Corp business.

The airport stuff he could do without, but the business side of things? Usually he thrived on it. Not this week. This week sucked.

Big-time.

He'd handled problems non-stop—from insubordinate contractors to fluctuating market values, bank errors to threatened strikes.

He'd had a gutful.

His only consolation? Business problems kept his mind off problems of another kind: namely Gemma.

In that annoying time before drifting off to sleep, when his mind blanked, the memory of their last encounter would surface, ramming home the fact that the woman he loved didn't believe in him.

Sure, he'd stuffed up with not telling her sooner about

why he'd initially hired her and the newspaper publicity, but what sort of a cold, heartless woman flung a sincere declaration back in his face?

Okay, so she wasn't cold or heartless—far from it. But he couldn't believe she wouldn't give him a chance to explain.

He'd compulsively checked his phone for messages or e-mails the last few days, hopeful she'd relent and contact him. Nothing.

He'd deluded himself into believing it was probably better this way: clean break, no emotional fallout.

Yeah, right.

He was kidding himself.

Aside from the fact he had to see her in the business arena for the next few weeks, until her tender ran out, he couldn't pretend what they'd shared meant nothing.

He might have chosen to shut emotions out of his life for years, but now he'd let them in there was no turning back.

He'd never be like his dad, going through women like socks, but he could see the appeal of never staying with one woman long enough to get involved. Lack of emotional ties meant pain-free disentanglements. Something he had a feeling would definitely *not* apply to him and Gemma.

A dull ache resided between his brows and had done for the last few days. Pinching the bridge of his nose to stop it from escalating, he strode through the deserted hallways of Devlin Corp.

He wasn't in the mood for an all-nighter, but he needed something to take his mind off Gemma now he'd mentally conjured her again.

Annoyed he'd had another lapse, he flung open the door to his office. Stopped dead.

Gemma had managed to surprise him yet again.

She raised an eyebrow, looked him up and down. 'About time you showed up.'

Speechless, he stared at the woman he loved, chained to his desk, wearing grungy camouflage pants, a black T-shirt, ugly fuchsia jellyfish earrings and a smile that could tempt a saint.

Considering he'd seen what she had beneath those awful clothes, he sure as hell was no saint.

Several long seconds later, when he'd managed to quell the urge to run across the office and scoop her into his arms, he shut the door and covered the distance between them to stand less than a foot away.

Close enough to smell her light spring sunshine fragrance. Close enough to see the flicker of uncertainty behind the sass in her eyes. Close enough to touch her.

He wanted to touch her—boy, did he want to. But he couldn't afford to get distracted. Not when they had a few issues to sort out. Namely, did they have a future?

'How long have you been tied to that thing?'

She shrugged and the chains around her wrists rattled. 'About thirty minutes.'

'How did you—?'

'Denise let me in. She knew your estimated time of arrival. I said I had important business that couldn't wait.' A tiny line creased her brow. 'Considering she's probably seen that picture of us in the tabloids, like the rest of Melbourne, I'm guessing she didn't buy my business excuse.'

She'd given him the perfect opening line to dive into an explanation about that latest publicity shot, but he didn't take it. He wanted to know why she was here before putting himself on the line again.

'Why the chains?'

She'd captured his attention the first time she'd pulled that trick and it hadn't waned since.

'Because I thought you needed to be reminded of my whacky, insane personality, and factor that into the way I behaved the last time we were together.'

'Oh.'

So much for being the articulate consummate professional.

'If you promise to listen, I'll untie them.'

He liked having her tied up at his mercy, but voicing that particular opinion wouldn't get them anywhere except naked and hot—two things he'd like, but would do little to solve their problems.

'Go ahead.'

It was bad enough reining in his rampant impulse to devour her while she was hog-tied, but when she bent forward to slip the chains off her ankles and he glimpsed a flash of black lace at her cleavage he clenched his fists to stop from reaching for her.

Instead he headed for the discreet bar tucked away in a cabinet, poured himself a double shot of whisky and downed it straight. When he heard blissful silence, meaning she'd finished slipping out of those damn chains, he risked a glance over his shoulder.

'Want a drink?'

'No, thanks.'

She was fiddling with an earring, twisting it till the thing should have snapped.

'Can we talk?'

'Sure,' he managed to croak out, before clearing his throat and gesturing towards the modular suite forming an L in the far corner.

He waited for her to sit before choosing the sofa opposite. The double shot might have cleared his head momentarily, but he had a feeling sitting too close to Gemma would befuddle it faster than he could blink.

She sat with her hands clasped in her lap, shoulders squared, spine straight, as if someone had stuck a rod down the back of her T-shirt. It was so far at odds with the laid-back woman comfortable in her own skin he knew she had to be as nervous as he was.

'I want to apologise for freaking out on you when you told me about the publicity and why you hired me,' she said, staring at some point over his left shoulder. 'It came from left field and really shook me up.'

She took a deep breath, straining against the fabric on her T-shirt, and he maintained eye contact with great effort.

'I don't do relationships as a rule, and you're the first guy I've dated in a while, so I felt betrayed and confused and— Ah, hell, this is becoming long-winded.'

She tugged on both earrings, managing to twist off a tentacle or two.

'What I'm trying to say is I shouldn't have run like that. I wanted to call, but thought this apology warranted a face-to-face meeting.'

She finally looked at him, expecting an answer, but his mind blanked.

What could he say? That he'd had an awful week because he missed her so much it felt like a permanent ache lodged in his chest? That he'd given up on them? That even if they tried this again how would he know she wouldn't do a runner again at some point in the future?

He settled for the simplest response.

'I'm glad you're here.'

One eyebrow rose in a sceptical arch. 'Really? Because you don't look it.'

'I'm thrown, that's all.'

That wasn't all, and they both knew it.

'You're peed off at me.'

He could lie, try to smooth things over, but what would be the point? If they stood any chance it had to be truth all the way from now on. 'Guess it's not every day I tell a woman I love her and she flings it back in my face.'

She winced. 'That was tactless. Not one of my proudest moments.' Her fiddling fingers stilled and she raised a hesitant glance. 'Did you mean it?'

'I'm not in the habit of saying things I don't mean.'

Jeez, could he sound any more uptight and pompous if he tried? Yeah, he was angry with her, but he had to let it go. Or walk away. Something he couldn't imagine doing at this point.

'I—I thought you said it to get me to forgive you.'

The thought had struck him while mulling it over these last few days. *Had* he thrown it out there in desperation? For fear of losing her? He didn't think so. Then again, did he really have a clue what love was?

'Honestly? I haven't had good role models in the love stakes. My grandfather was a tyrant who showed affection with gruffness. And you know my mum upped and left when I was a kid. Dad equates love with the latest model he can sweet-talk into his bed. I date. I don't do love.'

Her shoulders sagged at his bluntness, but the defiance never left her eyes. 'I keep hoping you'll clarify that with *until now.*'

'Do you want me to?'

'I just want the truth,' she said, her weary tone echoing the tiredness seeping through him. 'It's something I haven't had too much of lately.'

'What—?'

'Just some stuff I've learned from my mum.' She took a deep breath and eyeballed him. 'Let me get this straight.

I've apologized. You've semi-forgiven me. You say you love me but you don't do love.' She held her hands out palm-up and shrugged. 'Where do we go from here?'

'Damned if I know,' he muttered, hating the confusion clouding his head.

He wanted to clear up this mess and move on, but he was tired and grumpy—and wary. Wary of taking a chance, wary of having it blow up in his face again, but most of all wary of the power she held over him.

He didn't like having someone else responsible for his happiness, didn't like depending on anyone. Yet in a short period of time he'd done just that, and while Gemma had come here to apologise she hadn't given him any clue as to *her* feelings.

He wanted to give her a definitive answer, but right now he was running on empty.

'My work here is done.' She stood so abruptly she banged her knee on the table. He instinctively reached out to touch it but she swiftly sidestepped. 'I came here to see where we stand. Guess I have my answer.'

He should have stopped her, should have blurted out his innermost thoughts and deepest fears. But that would involve taking a monumental risk—even bigger than the one he'd taken when assuming the CEO role at Devlin Corp.

Could he do it?

One look at her downturned mouth and shimmering eyes and slumped shoulders was all the incentive he needed.

'Gemma, wait—'

She didn't, and he watched her walk out through the door, taking a piece of him with her again.

Gemma made it to the lift before the tears burning the backs of her eyes fell. Of all the stubborn, emotionally repressed, uptight jerks she had to go and fall in love with *him.*

She'd known it had been a mistake from the start, had lowered her defences regardless. *Idiot.*

Slow-burning anger replaced her indignation. Anger at herself for reneging on her staunchly independent stance and getting emotionally involved.

Mistake. *Big* mistake.

Her tears evaporated as anger took hold, refusing to be ignored.

Who the hell did he think he was? Telling her he loved her, then retreating behind his austere front despite her taking a risk and coming here?

He wasn't the only emotionally repressed person around here. She saw one in the mirror every morning, but *she'd* managed to reach out. Why couldn't he?

Fuming, she dashed a hand across her eyes and punched at the button, willing the numbers to accelerate quickly so she could get the hell out of here.

'Gemma, wait!'

Damn. She jabbed at the button repeatedly, her heart sinking as the lift stuck on the tenth floor. Swearing, she eyed the fire escape and wondered if she could jog down eighteen flights of stairs even as a hand clamped on her shoulder, effectively ending her escape plans.

'Please, come back to the office—'

'Why? So you can sit there and pretend you don't care? No, thanks.'

He blanched. 'You need to hear the truth.'

She shrugged off his hand, but he didn't let her go so easily, grabbing both her upper arms, blocking her, giving her no option but to look up at him.

'The truth? After the charade you've been perpetuating? Like you'd know what *that* is.'

She scored a direct hit and shame shadowed his gutted gaze. 'Please, Gemma, just five minutes.'

She owed him nothing. Apart from a swift kick where those bull-ants really should have bitten.

'Give me one good reason why I should go back into that office with you.'

He had exactly one second to make his answer count.

'When I said I love you, it wasn't an excuse to justify what I did. I do. Love you. And I want a chance to show you how much.'

The lift pinged and the doors slid open.

She had two options. Walk away now and preserve what was left of her shredded heart. Or give this one last shot.

'I won't let you down again, I promise.'

Her chest constricted, making it difficult to breathe. Her dad had used to make promises all the time.

We'll build that go-kart on the weekend, Gem. Promise. We'll check out my new secret fishing spot on the bay next week. Promise. We'll go hiking at the Grampians next summer. Promise.

Her dad had kept every promise he'd ever made to her. Would Rory? She'd done so much with her dad—at the expense of her mum, so she'd learned.

Ironically, thinking of Coral cemented her decision.

Don't waste a minute of your life wishing you could change a situation without giving it a damn good shake-up first.

Her mum was right. She didn't want to spend the next few months, maybe a lifetime, regretting that she hadn't given this a shake-up.

Not wanting to give in too easily, she tilted her head up, silenced him with a haughty glare before he could plead again.

'Just so you know, if a guy breaks a promise to me I use these chains to lash him to a concrete block and drop him off the end of Station Pier.'

She rattled her bag for emphasis and the corners of his mouth curved.

'I'll keep that in mind,' he said, slipping a hand under her elbow and guiding her back to his office.

When she hesitated at the door his grip tightened, as if he expected her to bolt.

'We owe this to ourselves,' he said, his breath fanning her hair, tickling her scalp.

She nodded in agreement, but was nervous nonetheless. What could he possibly say to convince her to take a chance?

They entered the office and he spun to face her, but before he could speak she held up a hand. 'Start at the beginning and tell me everything. The truth this time.'

He frowned, his hand unsteady as he jammed it through his hair, ruffling his usually immaculate short back and sides.

'Devlin Corp had problems with protestors on our last big project. It almost ruined us. Dad was in charge up at Port Douglas. There was a huge fuss and negative media input, saying we were ravaging the rainforest and worse.'

'Were you?'

He tensed, started pacing. 'My father isn't a businessman. He didn't have a clue. Hired the wrong consultants, took shortcuts, didn't read the fine print. Whatever he touched, it was a mess.' He drew in a long breath, blew it out. 'I stepped in to clean it up.'

'Then I came along and you thought you'd use me to fend off similar potential problems?'

He had the grace to nod imperceptibly. 'You were so gung-ho at the start I wanted to get rid of you. Then I saw your pitch and it blew me away. I knew you'd be an asset to the project. Around the same time I saw another mention of my father in the papers...' He winced. 'It was all about timing. You were hell-bent on scoring the job to protect your father's land. I was hell-bent on protecting my project from my father.'

She couldn't fault his logic, but it didn't detract from the fact he'd unashamedly used her.

'You saw it as a win-win.' She wanted to jab a finger in his direction but was too afraid it would shake. 'The consummate businessman, thinking about the bottom dollar, screw emotions.'

Stricken, he locked his gaze on hers. 'I didn't expect to fall for you.'

'That must've mucked up your perfectly constructed plan. Tell me—that picture of us together at Portsea. What was that about?'

He shook his head. 'A mistake. The publicity highlighting your strengths was all I wanted in the papers. Some over-enthusiastic journo must've wanted a scoop and continued to tail you.'

'Nice.'

He held his hands out to her, palms up. 'I'm sorry. I should've told you the truth from the beginning.'

'Yeah, you should've.' She twisted an earring, deriving little comfort from her marine friend. 'I opened up to you, told you how Mum had made me feel, like I was never good enough. Then you go and do the same.'

Horror widened his eyes, but she held up her hand to stave off a response.

'You told me not to doubt myself, that I was amazing, then you belittled me by doing this. Do you know what it felt like? A double betrayal. I thought you really understood me, the first guy to ever do that, then I discovered it was a ruse to protect your precious bloody company.'

'My love for you was never a ruse,' he said, the anguish contorting his mouth not detracting from its sensuous curve. 'I would never fake anything like that.'

Resisting the urge to rub away the agonising ache over her heart, she headed for the door. 'Good to know, but it doesn't change a thing—'

'Marry me.'

She stopped dead and stared at him in disbelief.

'I know what you're thinking. Who wants to marry a boorish workaholic who spends his life worrying about his business, using the people he loves for it, and can't see the best thing that ever happened to him even when she chains herself to whatever's handy to grab his attention?'

He waved his hand around the office.

'See this? It was my life till I met you. I'd have done anything for the business, including risk losing you. Using you for publicity and good PR and to deter protestors. Stupid. Monumentally stupid. Not any more.'

He took her hand and dropped to one knee. She was too stunned to do anything but gape.

'I've stuffed up again, blurting that proposal like I blurted how much I love you.' He raised her hand to his lips and kissed the back. 'This time I'm doing it right. I love you, Gemma. Love your quirkiness and exuberance and your conviction in standing up for what you believe in. Love you for who you are, inside and out. Love how you've opened my eyes in so many ways. Love how you make me feel a better man when I'm with you.'

He turned her hand over and kissed her palm, sending dizzying warmth spiralling through her.

'I'm hoping you can forgive me for stuffing up and not

telling you the truth earlier. I'm hoping you can believe in me. Enough to be my wife.'

Gemma stared at the man she loved kneeling in front of her, genuine love radiating from his eyes.

To see this strong, powerful, commanding man vulnerable to her made her realise she wasn't the only one with insecurities. When it came to love, it made nervous ninnies of them all.

'An answer some time this century would be nice, before I chain myself to a concrete block.'

She tugged on his hand, waiting till he stood before flinging herself into his arms, savouring the security of being held by the man she'd thought she'd lost.

He hugged her tight, mirroring her desire to never let go. She'd hold him to that.

When he released her, an eternity later, she stared into his incredible blue eyes, needing no further assurances.

People like them, who didn't trust their feelings, didn't open up easily. She believed him when he said he'd wanted to tell her the truth earlier, probably at that tiny café when she'd asked him not to spoil the moment.

But he'd opened up to her in every other way that counted, and to have the unswerving love of a guy like him...? She'd be a fool to walk away from what they could have.

While his declaration had been amazing, and she'd needed to hear him articulate his feelings, she should have trusted the depth of his love all along—for no one could fake the emotion shining from his eyes.

'So?'

She cupped his face. 'So I'm thinking October would be perfect for a spring wedding.'

He let out a jubilant whoop, picked her up and swung her around until they were breathless.

Rory pulled an all-nighter.

Gemma didn't mind. She was right there by his side, and work was the furthest thing from their minds.

EPILOGUE

'I NOW pronounce Portsea Point officially open.'

As the mayor cut the ribbon across the main road leading into the precinct, Rory squeezed Gemma's hand.

She glanced up at her husband and smiled through her tears.

Today had been bittersweet in so many ways: walking through the houses which would soon be filled with laughter and cooking aromas and squabbling siblings, touring her dad's land where the newly built marine preservation park would soon be enjoyed by families and tourists and anyone with a passion for this beautiful beach.

Rory and Devlin Corp had come through for her, constructing the conservation area exactly the way she'd envisaged, and she hoped the people who lived here would love this place as much as her dad had.

'Let's get out of here.'

Rory tugged on her hand and she didn't need encouragement to follow his lead. He'd done his duty, making an inspiring speech before the mayor. Besides, she knew where he was leading her.

Their spot.

They slipped through the crowd and turned left, walking in silence till they reached the end of the road where it opened into a car park. A huge wooden sign hung over the entrance.

KARL SHULTZ MEMORIAL PARK. The words had been carved into the wood by a local craftsman, and her throat constricted as it always did when she saw the evidence of how much her husband loved her.

They didn't speak. Rory allowed her time to absorb the significance of this as he always did, respecting her need for private memories as she silently connected with her dad.

They walked through the sand-gravel mix to the entrance of the park—a sprawling acre edged by a natural ti-tree border. There was no sea wall that would have long-term disastrous consequences for the beach beyond.

There was no newfangled plastic play equipment or electric barbecue here. Just rudimentary wooden climbing frames and benches, and that spectacular view over the ocean—a view she'd treasured from the first time she'd camped here at seven years of age.

They stood on the edge of the park, hand in hand, and her heart swelled with love for this man who understood her and accepted her and loved her unconditionally.

He'd put up with her buying an old house in Kew and renovating it to six-star energy efficiency, he'd tolerated her chickens taking up the sole corner of their back yard that hadn't been converted into a veggie patch, and he hadn't blinked when she'd taken up the next greatest environmental cause and spent two months in the Gulf of Carpentaria.

He let her be herself while demonstrating his love in so many ways. When she woke before him each morning and watched him sleep, his mouth relaxed, his eyelashes shadowing his cheeks, she wondered what she'd done to deserve him.

'How can I ever thank you for doing this? For merging our dreams for the land together and creating harmony? For understanding how much preserving the marine area here meant to me? For everything?'

He touched her earring—a platinum killer whale with a twinkling diamond eye—and smiled.

'The day you agreed to marry me was thanks enough.'

'That's incredibly corny.'

Adorably bashful, he shrugged. 'What can I say? I'm a novice in this love business.'

'Lucky for us, we can learn as we go along.'

Sliding her hands around his neck, she lowered his head and kissed him.

Perfect.

When her husband kissed like a dream she could quite happily look forward to a lifetime of hands-on practice in the love stakes.

* * * * *

Mills & Boon® Hardback

February 2012

ROMANCE

HISTORICAL

MEDICAL

ROMANCE

The Most Coveted Prize	Penny Jordan
The Costarella Conquest	Emma Darcy
The Night that Changed Everything	Anne McAllister
Craving the Forbidden	India Grey
Her Italian Soldier	Rebecca Winters
The Lonesome Rancher	Patricia Thayer
Nikki and the Lone Wolf	Marion Lennox
Mardie and the City Surgeon	Marion Lennox

HISTORICAL

Married to a Stranger	Louise Allen
A Dark and Brooding Gentleman	Margaret McPhee
Seducing Miss Lockwood	Helen Dickson
The Highlander's Return	Marguerite Kaye

MEDICAL

The Doctor's Reason to Stay	Dianne Drake
Career Girl in the Country	Fiona Lowe
Wedding on the Baby Ward	Lucy Clark
Special Care Baby Miracle	Lucy Clark
The Tortured Rebel	Alison Roberts
Dating Dr Delicious	Laura Iding

Mills & Boon® Hardback
March 2012

ROMANCE

Roccanti's Marriage Revenge	Lynne Graham
The Devil and Miss Jones	Kate Walker
Sheikh Without a Heart	Sandra Marton
Savas's Wildcat	Anne McAllister
The Argentinian's Solace	Susan Stephens
A Wicked Persuasion	Catherine George
Girl on a Diamond Pedestal	Maisey Yates
The Theotokis Inheritance	Susanne James
The Good, the Bad and the Wild	Heidi Rice
The Ex Who Hired Her	Kate Hardy
A Bride for the Island Prince	Rebecca Winters
Pregnant with the Prince's Child	Raye Morgan
The Nanny and the Boss's Twins	Barbara McMahon
Once a Cowboy...	Patricia Thayer
Mr Right at the Wrong Time	Nikki Logan
When Chocolate Is Not Enough...	Nina Harrington
Sydney Harbour Hospital: Luca's Bad Girl	Amy Andrews
Falling for the Sheikh She Shouldn't	Fiona McArthur

HISTORICAL

Untamed Rogue, Scandalous Mistress	Bronwyn Scott
Honourable Doctor, Improper Arrangement	Mary Nichols
The Earl Plays With Fire	Isabelle Goddard
His Border Bride	Blythe Gifford

MEDICAL

Dr Cinderella's Midnight Fling	Kate Hardy
Brought Together by Baby	Margaret McDonagh
The Firebrand Who Unlocked His Heart	Anne Fraser
One Month to Become a Mum	Louisa George

Mills & Boon® Large Print
March 2012

ROMANCE

The Power of Vasilii	Penny Jordan
The Real Rio D'Aquila	Sandra Marton
A Shameful Consequence	Carol Marinelli
A Dangerous Infatuation	Chantelle Shaw
How a Cowboy Stole Her Heart	Donna Alward
Tall, Dark, Texas Ranger	Patricia Thayer
The Boy is Back in Town	Nina Harrington
Just An Ordinary Girl?	Jackie Braun

HISTORICAL

The Lady Gambles	Carole Mortimer
Lady Rosabella's Ruse	Ann Lethbridge
The Viscount's Scandalous Return	Anne Ashley
The Viking's Touch	Joanna Fulford

MEDICAL

Cort Mason – Dr Delectable	Carol Marinelli
Survival Guide to Dating Your Boss	Fiona McArthur
Return of the Maverick	Sue MacKay
It Started with a Pregnancy	Scarlet Wilson
Italian Doctor, No Strings Attached	Kate Hardy
Miracle Times Two	Josie Metcalfe